CRIMSON

Mage

OTHER BOOKS BY DOROTHY DREYER

Phoenix Descending

Paragon Rising

Cauldron of Ash

Christmas in Silverwood

THE EMPIRE OF THE LOTUS SERIES

Crimson Mage

Copper Mage

Golden Mage

Emerald Mage

Sapphire Mage

Amethyst Mage

Diamond Mage

CRIMSON

Mage

EMPIRE OF THE LOTUS

BOOK ONE

DOROTHY DREYER

Crimson Mage
Empire of the Lotus Book One
Third Edition

ISBN: 978-1-948661-41-6

Published January 2020 by Snowy Wings Publishing
PO Box 1035, Turner, OR 97392

www.snowywingspublishing.com

*For my faithful companions
on this ever-changing journey*

Upon the one hundredth reincarnation of the Lotus empress, the dark god Kashmeru would send out his shadow army—Pishacha—to destroy the reborn empress, which in turn would bring about the collapse of the universe.

The world changed at the time of the Eradication. The New Asian Administration outlawed mages, forbidding any use of their powers. To protect her imprisoned family, Mayhara Guatama made a deal to surrender her mage status and pledge her life to the New Order.

Years have passed, the chaos from the upheaval long since settled. Or so Mayhara believed... until she receives a mysterious message pleading for her help.

Stunned by the claim that the empress has been reincarnated, Mayhara must choose between fealty to the Lotus empire, or honoring the decree that assured her family's safety.

It is courage, courage, courage,
that raises the blood of life to
crimson splendor. Live bravely and
present a brave front to adversity.
—Horace

The legend goes …

The ancient deity Kashmeru knew only one true love—the Lotus empress Lakshmi, who in his eyes possessed all beauty and grace the universe could hold. Their hearts called to one another, a hold so strong that neither one could deny the bond. But Lakshmi knew that Kashmeru's spirit was not pure, for an evil dwelled within his soul, a wickedness so corrupt that it could destroy the universe.

And when she denied him her love, destroying the universe was the very thing he vowed to do.

Throughout the centuries, their reincarnations were drawn to one another, but the outcome was always the same: Lakshmi would never give Kashmeru her heart.

To put an end to his constant chase, the Empire of the Lotus defeated Kashmeru and sealed him in a tomb using mage powers, where he would remain trapped …

… until the Council of the Seven could secure the blood of the Lotus empress to set him free.

One

Mayhara swore that if her ComLinq buzzed one more time, she'd hurl it through her computer monitor. Her fingers danced near the device, itching to grab it if it dared to make another sound. She inhaled deeply, cautioning herself to calm down.

Breathe in for four seconds. Hold for seven. Calmly exhale for eight.

She knew she wouldn't actually chuck the device; not only would she probably lose her job, but it would take forever to set up a new ComLinq, especially since she hadn't backed up her data for at least a month. Plus, it was unlike her to lose her cool like that. No. If Rajev had sent her another message, she would simply remove him from her contacts—which she should have done the moment she'd found out he'd logged into her bank account and transferred a thousand of her merits to his account. She didn't need to see another apology message or another excuse that he'd simply been borrowing the credit. She didn't believe him, and she couldn't trust him. No matter how many times he told her he loved her. Still, though she'd been quick to change her banking passwords, she hadn't yet blocked him from her Linq.

Breathe in for four seconds. Hold for seven. Calmly exhale for eight.

She was fooling herself if she thought she could actually hold her breath for seven seconds. Instead of the usual four-seven-eight, she opted for her more realistic four-five-six.

Cringing, she ignored the slight burn in her chest, refusing to believe it was heartache. Rajev wasn't worth it.

It was probably just the curry she'd had for lunch. She took a sip of her bottled water and punched in the numbers for the next file she needed to process. She may have been down a thousand merits in her bank account, but she'd be damned if her stupid boyfriend—*ex-boyfriend*, actually—would cause her to fall behind in her work.

As the names and numbers on her screen began to blur in her vision, Mayhara took another slow, deep breath. She closed her eyes, calling upon the meditation technique she'd learned when she'd been training back at the mage academy—the very academy the government had all but forced her to forget about. She cringed at the heartbreaking memory of the academy's shutdown, the brutal invasion of the government forces, the outrageous law that announced that mages were now outlawed. The system that had stripped her of her identity. The only reason she was sitting at this desk doing government work rather than sitting in a prison camp starving to death was because she had agreed to give up chakra magic and become a pawn on the New Asian Administration's side of the law. And she had only done that to ensure the safety of her family.

Her fingers immediately went to the back of her neck, feeling the small scar that had been left when the government had implanted their blocking device. That was what they called it—a *blocking* device—but it didn't block mage powers at all. Instead, upon detecting mage powers being used, the device would send shockwaves of painful electricity to the implantee's nerve endings, causing enough pain that the mage would cease using their powers. When the mage stopped using those powers, the blocker would stop sending the shockwaves.

Cut it out. You've got work to do.

She opened her eyes and shook off the memory. There was nothing she could do about her old life now. She had no choice but to move forward. Darshana—her guru at the academy—had always taught her to hold on to positivity. To concentrate on any happy little thought she could find in her subconscious, anything that brought her even the smallest amount of joy. To think about that and only that for seventeen seconds. Doing so should bring a similar happy thought, and so on and so on, until the universe had no choice but to match that vibration and deliver something equally positive.

Darshana had said it could be as simple as enjoying

the sound of rain or smiling at a cat licking its paw to clean its face.

She had a nice flat in the upper end of New Jaipur—one of the most sought-after places to live after the chaos of the East Asian Unification—she made a generous salary, and her two-year probationary job trial was almost complete, meaning she would soon secure an official position at the Citizen Census Processing Centre. All this at the age of nineteen; not every young woman in New United Asia was this lucky.

To hell with Rajev! She was better off without him.

"Hey, Mayha."

The voice from her office door pulled her out of her thoughts. She glanced up at Riya, who leaned against the door frame with her arms crossed over her tight sweater. Mayhara did her best to offer her friend a smile.

"Doing any better?" Riya leaned her head forward as she said it, lowering her voice. "Or do I have to kick you-know-who's ass?"

Mayhara appreciated that Riya knew not to spread the news about Rajev and his wrongdoings. The last thing she needed was rumors circulating about how naïve she was, especially before her promotion was finalized.

"I'm absolutely fine," she said, keeping her chin up. "That piece of scum isn't even worth a second of thought. I've got more important things to concentrate on. Why do you ask?"

"Because that 'piece of scum' keeps texting me to ask if you're getting his messages."

It took all Mayhara's energy to not roll her eyes. Instead, she focused her attention on her monitor. "Let him wonder."

Riya pushed herself off the doorframe, checking over her shoulder before approaching Mayhara's desk. "It's a shame. He was cute. I thought maybe you two would settle down together."

Mayhara almost laughed. Her relationship with Rajev had begun because they'd had something to commiserate over, namely missing their families. Except Rajev's family was in another country because of the business they ran, not because they were locked up in a prison camp. And that made it even more infuriating; he *knew* she was saving up to support her family once she'd be able to petition for their release. He knew how much she needed the credit, and he stole it anyway.

It was for the better that their relationship ended

anyway. She had to put her family first. She shook her head at Riya. "I'm too young to settle down. Not in a serious, ready-for-marriage kind of way, at least."

"Right." Riya smoothed the material of her skirt. "I keep forgetting you're only nineteen. Feels like you've been here for ages."

Mayhara held back a sigh. The truth was, it felt like ages to her as well. She'd been seized by the government when she'd been a mere seventeen, sacrificing everything to keep her family safe. Everything she'd ever known had been stolen from her: her scheduled training at the mage academy, her home, her parents, her sisters, her guru. Even her sense of self. In order to survive, she'd become what the government had wanted her to become.

A *ping* on her monitor snapped her out of her thoughts. Her nerves tensed for a moment, fearing that Rajev had found a way to hack into her work's server. Then she realized that rather than another message from Rajev, it was an interoffice notification.

"What is it?" Riya asked.

"Director Shei's secretary. Shei wants to see me."

Riya's eyes lit up. "Maybe she's promoting you early!"

Mayhara bit back a hopeful smile. "It could be

anything." She stood and worried the collar of her blouse, making her way toward the door.

"Before you go…" Riya had a sheepish look on her face. "I need to ask you a favor."

"Sure, what is it?"

"Decon finally took the hint and asked me out."

"Came to his senses, did he?"

"Yeah. Thing is, I've been trying to figure out what to wear. And… you know that red dress you wore to last year's charity event?" Riya bit her lip.

"You want to borrow it?"

"Could I?"

Mayhara let out a small laugh, nodding her head. The only reason she owned the dress was because her boss had insisted she wear something appropriate. The charity event had had a strict dress code. "Of course. What time do you want to pick it up?"

"We're going to dinner at seven, so I'll need to come by… at the latest six? Five-thirty would be better."

"Oh. I'm not sure I'll be home by then." She rubbed at her arm, considering giving Riya the key code to her flat. Normally, she wouldn't have thought twice about it, but seeing as how the guy she had been in a relationship with had practically robbed her recently, she had a moment of doubt.

Riya flashed her a curious look. "Mayha?"

Mayhara shook her head, telling herself not to let Rajev's treacherous behavior affect all her decisions. "I'll linq you my key code if I'm not done by then."

Riya clasped her hands together, a huge smile plastered on her face. "Thank you, Mayha! You're the best. I promise I'll just be in and out. I just need the dress. It's going to make the evening so much better."

"Then I hope you have lots of fun." Mayhara shoved her Linq in her blazer pocket. "I better go before Shei pops a vein."

Mayhara made her way down the hall to the elevator, her heels clicking along the marble floor. The high-tech building's built-in sensors lit up her path as she maneuvered down the long hallway. When she reached the elevator, the doors opened without her having to push any buttons, the soft swish of it like a whisper, and the computer's voice welcomed her by name.

"Twenty-eight, please," Mayhara instructed.

The elevator doors closed smoothly. Director Shei's office was on the top floor of the twenty-eight-story building, so Mayhara had about a half a minute on the elevator to try to compose herself. If she got the promotion early, she might be able to petition to get her family out of the holding camp before the month was over. Her eyes brimmed with tears at the thought of being able to see her family again, to finally have them come live with her. She wouldn't be able to get them all out at once, but one-by-one, they'd be together again.

"Floor twenty-eight," the computer informed her.

As the elevator doors slid open, Mayhara blew out a calming breath and held her chin up. She couldn't show weakness or uncertainty. She had to come across as self-assured and confident.

Pai-han, Director Shei's secretary, stood as Mayhara approached, his form slender in his button-up white shirt and black slacks. He gave her a slight bow, which she returned, then gestured to a chair nearby.

"Director Shei will see you momentarily," Pai-han said. "Can I offer you some matcha?" His fingers hovered over the control pad on his desk, ready to click in an order.

Offering tea was a good sign. Mayhara's shoulders relaxed a bit. "No, thank you."

"Very well." He abandoned the control pad and

gestured again to the chair. "Please have a seat."

She sat in the plush chair, clearing her throat. Though she felt impatient to find out why she was being called to the director's office, she was relieved to have a couple more minutes to compose herself. If she could just stop the sweat from forming at her temples, she might be all right.

Director Shei's office door opened, making Mayhara jolt upright. There was no chance to stop the sweating now.

Shiny silver buttons on a blue-grey, synthetic wool uniform—and an affixed badge sporting the New United Asia emblem—caught her eye. It was a law enforcement officer who'd stepped out of Shei's office, and Mayhara's brow furrowed. The officer turned to bow to Director Shei, who'd followed him out of her office, looking pristine and polished, her hair in a tight bun and her dress suit appearing freshly pressed.

The officer's eyes roamed toward Mayhara for a split second before reverting back to the director. "We'll be in touch," he said.

"Thank you, officer." She didn't smile or bow her head to him. She simply watched him leave for a moment before turning toward Mayhara. "Miss Guatama, you may enter my office now."

Mayhara stood and straightened her clothes, following her boss into the office. Inside, her eyes immediately went to the view of the city from Director Shei's panorama windows. It was incredible to see. The sun had started to set, spreading bursts of pink and orange through the sky and prompting the city buildings to darken into silhouettes. She had to stop herself from gaping at the sight and instead settled herself into the chair across from her boss's enormous desk. The feel of the cold leather brought back memories of herself at seventeen, sitting in the very same chair, being forced to choose between working for the government or being sent to a prison camp. She'd been terrified then, and somehow, her feelings in the present moment weren't that different.

"I hope I didn't tear you away from an important project," Director Shei said, straightening a stack of papers on her desk.

"No, Director." Mayhara fought to not fidget. "I was actually glad you called me to your office."

Shei raised a perfectly-plucked brow. "Oh? Why is that?"

Mayhara blanched. She found it hard to move her lips

correctly. Struggling to find her voice, she wiped her sweaty palms on her skirt and shook her head. "What I mean is… I'm always available for whatever you need."

"Hmm." Shei studied her for a moment and then leaned forward on her desk. "I have an important assignment for you. I hope you are diligent enough to attend to the task."

"Of course, Director."

Shei spoke slowly and concisely. "It seems the political unrest in the prison camps of Old Bombay is rising."

Director Shei pushed a button on the side of her desk, and the blinds on the windows began to lower. Sliding open one of her desk drawers, she pulled out a long cylinder tube. It was made of a shiny black material, and the ends were adorned with red tassels. Shei pushed a small silver button at one end of the tube, which omitted a beep. The tube opened, and Shei pulled out a scroll.

Mayhara inched forward in her seat as Shei unrolled the scroll over her desk. Shei spread her hand and dragged it along the electronic map of New United Asia. Bordered areas on the map lit up in bright blue lines on the electronic paper, and a series of red flashing dots were spread out in random spots. "These blue areas are the prison camps. The red you see are where accounts of rebellious behavior have been reported. At first the numbers were low, but the incidents are now climbing, and word is these radicals have formed a wide-spread band of mercenaries with the intention of waging war on the New Asian Administration."

"Is that why the Imperial Police were here? Are you being threatened?"

"It hasn't come to that, no. But the Imperial Police do want our assistance."

Mayhara hesitated. Something in her gut twisted. Though she couldn't claim to be of the same opinion as radicals, the people in those camps were her people. She narrowed her eyes at something on the map that caught her attention. "What are the black triangles?"

Shei seemed to tighten her jaw before offering the slightest of smiles. She rolled up the map and returned it to the cylinder. "Nothing to be concerned about. But the Imperial Police have been brainstorming ideas to deter the mercenaries and have come to us with one of their strategies."

"What do they need?"

"Leverage. The radicals must have families, close friends, people on the outside they associate with."

Mayhara swallowed hard. "Do the police mean to extort the radicals by threatening their families?"

Director Shei's expression became colder than usual. "It's not our business how the law deals with them. It's just our duty to assist them."

"H-How? What do you need me to do?"

"You work with the census records. I need you to track down the radicals' families."

"That could take the whole weekend."

"Do you have a problem with that?"

Mayhara was about to answer when she felt a vibration in her blazer pocket. Before logic could tell her to ignore it, she slipped out her Linq, low enough that Director Shei could not see, and glanced at the screen.

The Lotus is in danger. Meet me at the loop. 7 P.M. -GD

Mayhara blinked, unable to wrap her head around the message. She didn't recognize the number the message was from, but the mention of the "Lotus" and asking to meet at the "loop" meant it could only be one person.

Especially with the initials GD.

Guru Darshana?

She hadn't heard from her guru since the school had been shut down. In fact, she doubted Darshana had ever had a ComLinq. It seemed unlikely she would have one now, but still…

The twisting in Mayhara's gut grew more intense, and her palms began to tingle. Her mage powers called out to her, and she then realized that it was why she'd started to feel pain. The device implanted in her neck was programmed to inflict pain if it sensed her powers being used. But this call for help was something the root of her being could not ignore. Her mage energy was naturally magnetized to her guru's beckon.

"Miss Guatama," Director Shei said, the authority in her voice almost palpable. "Please answer my question. Do you have a problem with my request?"

Mayhara squeezed her hands shut, trying to shut off the power. She opened her mouth, but no sound escaped.

Director Shei narrowed her eyes. "Do I have to remind you that the review for your official position with the government will be taking place soon? Your compliance in this assignment would do well to sway the board members in your favor."

And having that official position was what she needed to see her family again.

"No, Director Shei. I don't have a problem with it." Mayhara struggled to keep her hands shut. Her nails dug into her palms, making her want to wince. Still, she kept a straight face. "Of course I'll help."

"Very well." There was a hint of the smallest smile on the director's face. She rolled up the map and placed the scroll back in its tube. "Don't stay too late tonight. I'd prefer it if you were alert and at your best to work the entire day tomorrow."

Mayhara nodded absently.

"That will be all. Thank you for your service."

Mayhara stood and gave her boss a curt bow before leaving the office. She walked past Pai-han in a daze. It felt like forever before she reached the elevator. Once inside, she opened her hands. Small molecules of sparkling, crimson energy burst from her palms, clouding the elevator. Mayhara waved her hands around to clear the dust, ignoring the ache in her neck, and then whipped out her Linq to reread the message.

A cold shiver ran over her body. She winced as the

pinpricks of pain shot through her. But the ComLinq message overwhelmed her more. The Lotus was in danger? How could that be possible? She hadn't even been aware the empress had been reborn.

Two

*L*akshmi.

Naree opened her eyes. His voice caressed her like velvet. He was still with her. He'd never left.

"Kashmeru?"

Yes, my love. I'm waiting for you.

Naree turned her head, her cheek brushing against

the silky pillow. This was not her bed. She could barely remember how she ended up in this apartment. All she knew was she was pulled here, as if some magical force had a hold of her heart and wouldn't let go until she followed where it led.

Lakshmi, I need you.

It wasn't the name she went by in this life, but it was her name once. Still. Deep inside of her, she was still Lakshmi.

"I can't," she said. "We can't be together. I should go home."

I am your home, my love.

"No." A tear escaped and slid down her cheek, for her heart did not agree with her words. She longed to be with him as much as he longed to be with her.

Come to me. I will show you.

She closed her eyes, letting the tears come.

Three

Mayhara stayed off the well-lit city streets, and the black jeans and dark grey hoodie helped her blend into the shadows of the night. Getting to the underground station wasn't the tricky part, though. The tricky part would be catching the sub-train without anyone noticing her. But she had to take the risk; there was no other way of finding out if the message she'd received was really from her guru.

Before she'd ventured out into the dark of night, Mayhara had linqed Riya the key code to her flat and placed the dress she'd wanted to borrow near the front door so she wouldn't have to go searching for it. Her anxiousness about whether or not Riya would get in or if she'd remember to lock up once she left slowly dissipated the closer Mayhara got to the sub-train station. Instead, her thoughts were geared more toward why the Lotus empress might be in trouble, when the new empress had been reborn, and why Mayhara herself was being called to help.

She pulled her hood over her head as she got to the station and kept her shoulders hunched. Mages were outlawed, and though riding the sub-train wasn't an illegal act, she could run into trouble if anyone found out she was going to her old training academy.

Especially because it was located on the palace grounds.

She kept her head down until the sub-train pulled into the station, averting her gaze from the people on the platform and the passengers already on the train. Her shoulders remained hunched as she slipped into an empty seat. Her skin tingled, and she couldn't get past the feeling she was being watched. A guy in a black trench coat loitered by the train doors with his hands in his pockets. Fighting the acidic feeling in her stomach, she averted her eyes when he looked her way. She glanced at the route map on the sub-train monitor, noting that she needed to wait seven more stops before she reached her destination. It was something she actually had memorized, but counting down the stations somehow kept her calm.

The man lurking by the door shifted his position, leaning on the opposite side of the door frame and taking his Linq out of his pocket. She told herself not to be paranoid, that the man was probably not linqing anyone about her being on the train. As they approached the next station, it crossed her mind to get off, to see if he would follow her, but when the train pulled to a stop, the man exited and went on his way.

She let out a sigh of relief. The government was controlling, but she wasn't sure if they would go so far as to monitor her Linq messages. Of course, if they did, it was highly unlikely they would know what the "loop" was. Plus, if they were hell bent on keeping her away from finding out about the Lotus empress, they would be sure to have her followed. Yet everyone she'd been suspicious of on the train so far had departed.

Stop after stop, people exited the sub-train, much too concerned about finally getting home after a busy day to pay her any attention. The train ascended from its underground route to one above ground. They were out of the city now and traveling through the countryside on the outskirts. Her muscles loosened, and she began to relax in her seat, focusing instead on the scenery outside her window, even as dark as it was. It had been two years since she'd been to the palace. Two years since she'd been ripped out of the training academy on the palace grounds. She was both excited to see it again and fearful of the state it might be in after the Eradication soldiers had ambushed it.

One stop before hers, she was left alone on the train. She glanced around, spotting the security cameras and wondering if the train driver found it odd that she would be traveling so far. After all, there was nothing out here but the abandoned palace. She pulled her hood tighter over her head, hoping the cameras hadn't caught too much footage of her.

She stood as the train started to slow and headed toward the door. With her hands hidden in her jacket pockets, she exited the train and trudged toward the path that led to the palace.

Like a land of respite, the giant structure of the palace, which could be seen past the sturdy cast-iron fence standing sentry around the grounds, was surrounded by once-well-tended-to gardens, now abandoned and left to wither. There was apparent damage to the buildings that made up the different wings of the palace, but still it stood, holding strong like a sturdy skeleton whose flesh and guts had been beaten and ripped apart. Mayhara gasped as she drew closer, hardly remembering the piles of rubble and shards of broken stained glass littering the imperial property.

As she pushed open the unlocked gate, her heart felt heavy, as if it too had been partially demolished with the place she had once called home.

The fact that it was abandoned—and that no one seemed to be around for miles—made her think that the government had no further use for the palace, now that it was destroyed, and had left it untouched after the ambush.

Even in the darkness, Mayhara could make out the different areas of the palace: the guard stations, the mediation center, the jogging path for the students, the gazebo where they held special summer events, the zen statues, and fountains. She was glad not all of it was destroyed.

She made her way toward the palace entrance. The large double doors had been knocked down during the ambush, so there would be no problem getting in. Her heart raced with anticipation to see the familiar hall that had welcomed her so many years ago. The emptiness of the place surprised her; she had never seen the palace so vacant in all her years attending the mage academy. Though she spent more time in the classrooms and the training halls, the students of the academy frequented the palace on more occasions than she could name. Somehow, even empty, it felt as if it were filled with magic. Even the dust floating through the palace seemed to carry a magical element, as if it were still holding on to hope that the empire would be restored.

She checked the time on her Linq and pushed forward. The main hall led straight back, where she found the door that went out to the courtyard between the palace and the school. Weeds and debris covered the once-pristine sandstone path in the courtyard. The sound of her shoes crunching along through the dead leaves made her uneasy, as if she were disturbing a place of peace.

She passed a wooden bench under a tall Sakura tree, and her chest throbbed with the memory of spending free periods with her friends there. She wrapped an arm around her stomach, which roiled with the ache of being torn away from them all. She'd barely spoken any of their names since that day. Though it had been a time of anticipation—a period of time when the entire empire had waited for the reincarnation of the Lotus empress—Mayhara and her friends had still been honored to be a part of the mage academy, training to defend the long-awaited empress, whenever she was fated to appear.

In front of the school, she took in the sight of the broken windows and overturned desks that had made their way out onto the lawn because of the attack. A shiver trembled through her as she fought the terror of the memory. She and her friends had been shocked. A few classmates and teachers had even died trying to fight back. If they had been prepared, perhaps they could have held their ground, but it had been an ambush—the Eradication, the government had called it—and they hadn't stood a chance.

They had all been detained, separated, and worst of

all, they'd been confused. All Mayhara had known was that everyone she knew and loved was being threatened. The government had given her a choice, and in the end, she'd chosen to keep her family alive.

Tears brimmed in Mayhara's eyes. The memories that flooded back were like a tsunami of pain and sorrow. She shook her head, forcing the thoughts away. She was here for a reason, and she needed to hurry up and find out why. She needed to find out if the message she'd received was truly from her former guru.

She turned on her heel, facing away from the school building, and headed toward the combat field. Stone tiles were lined up in a circular pattern. This was where they'd done most of their mage training. Mayhara's palms grew hot just from being here.

She made her way to the center of the stones. Senses on high alert, she held her arms away from her body, palms down. For a moment, she hesitated, curious and a bit afraid that she'd been set up. Well, if she had, she would deal with it. There was no turning back now.

She closed her eyes and let her magic be free. A warm thrill spiraled through her, and she couldn't hold back the smile from finally feeling the exhilaration of allowing her mage powers to surface. Her blocker kicked in and sent electric pulses through her body. At first, she tensed up, letting out a groan from the pain. But she clenched her teeth together and pushed through the pain. She couldn't let that damned blocker stop her from finding out if her guru needed her help or if the Lotus empress had truly been reincarnated. What was a little pain compared to restoring peace to the world?

Okay, it was a bit more than a little pain. She squeezed her eyes shut and forced herself to fight through the pulsing ache in her veins.

Her hands grew hotter. She heard a shifting of stones.

Opening her eyes, she witnessed a sight she hadn't seen in years. A metal loop, eight feet in diameter, that lay within the pattern of the stones around her began to rotate. First in a circle around her until it sped up slightly and began to emit a red glow. And then one end of the loop lifted from the stones and into the air, the other end sinking into the earth, forming a vertical circle around her.

In the next moment, the stones around her seemed to drop into the ground, but they did so systematically, forming a spiral staircase that led downward beneath the surface of the ground. She smiled at the familiar sight, having at one time thought that she would never again be able to behold it. She waited until all the stones had shifted into place, and then she began her descent.

A feeling of nostalgia came over her as she descended into the dark underground chamber. Even running her hand along the railing brought back memories. As she reached the bottom of the staircase, she took in the sight of the huge training hall. The administration had not been aware of the space. It remained untouched. She felt relieved to know there was at least one place on the palace grounds the government hadn't decimated. The only sign of disturbance were small rocks and rubble that had fallen from the ceiling, evidently the fallout from the Eradication above-ground.

She took a few steps forward, scanning the area. The silence pushed in on her, and her palms began to tingle. Instinctively, she held them up, preparing herself.

"Darshana?"

From a dark corner of the space, a figure moved into the light. Mayhara's breath hitched as she realized it was not her guru, but some hooded man. His hoodie cast a shadow over his face, and she could barely make out his eyes.

I've been set up!

"Stop right there," she shouted, glowing crimson particles emanating from her palms, ready to do her bidding.

"You don't understand," the mysterious man said. He held up his hands.

Mayhara didn't have time to question whether he was about to unleash powers against her; she pushed her energy out.

Streams of rock-hard crimson particles flew through the air toward the man.

He ducked down to dodge them, rolled to the side, and then jumped up into a defensive position.

Mayhara charged at him, ready to hit him with another blast of crimson.

Instead of backing away, he swooped down, low to the ground, and knocked her off her feet.

She twisted as she fell, rolling to her side and pushing herself up. She swung her arm as if pitching a ball, and a glowing sphere of crimson coursed through the air. It hit him in the shoulder, knocking him down.

Not taking a chance that he would be down for long, Mayhara rushed toward him, palms up.

"Wait," came a voice from behind her.

Mayhara froze, nearly tripping as she skidded to a stop. Palms still up, she swiveled around to face the source of the voice.

"Darshana!"

The old woman raised a brow. "Long time, no annoying red dust."

Mayhara opened her mouth to respond, but the room spun in on her from shock. She stumbled backward, barely catching herself before she fell.

"Don't kill the boy, dear," Darshana said. "You need to listen to him."

Four

Mayhara slowly lowered her hands. She felt the tingle of the glow fade to nothing by the time her hands reached her thighs.

With wide eyes, she took in the sight of her former guru. She hadn't changed much, save for a few more strands of grey hair. For someone nearing sixty—or was it seventy?—Darshana had an amazing complexion; she hardly had any wrinkles. Her form was petite, and though

Mayhara had already been a head taller than her the last time they'd seen each other, she towered even higher over her now that Darshana had developed a slight hunch to her back.

Mayhara couldn't stop the smile spreading across her face. She quickly placed her feet together, made a fist with one hand, laid a flat palm over the fist with her other hand, and gave Darshana a respectful bow. As soon as she straightened back up, she ran toward her guru and threw her arms around her.

"Darshana, it feels like forever."

Darshana stroked the back of Mayhara's head once. "Time is but an illusion, my crimson petal."

Mayhara backed up, studying her guru in wonder. "What is happening? I'm so confused. I wasn't even sure that message was from you."

Darshana tucked her hands into her long, wide sleeves and nodded. "It was from me. We have come to a difficult circumstance, and the world needs your help."

"The world?" Mayhara shook her head. "But—Why me? And what does this guy have to do with it?"

The man cleared his throat, moving into the shaft of light that snuck through the cracks of the ceiling. He nonchalantly pulled his hood off his head.

Mayhara studied him, squinting her eyes. "Wait. I … I know you, don't I? I remember you from school. Jaehyun?"

"I wondered when you would recognize me." He leaned forward, sticking his hands in his pockets. "But, please, it's just 'Jae.'"

"Jae. Right. You've… uh, filled out." As soon as Mayhara said it, she felt a hot blush spread across her cheeks.

Jae rubbed at his shoulder—the shoulder where she'd hit him with crimson energy, she realized. "Yeah, so have you."

As a flush crept across her cheeks, she turned her attention to Darshana. "Uh, so what's this all about?"

Jae took a deep breath and gave Darshana a look. Mayhara narrowed her eyes at her guru, her curiosity at its peak.

"It's about the Lotus empress. She's in danger."

"That's what your message said." Mayhara shook her head again, still not grasping the reality of the situation. "I didn't know she'd been reincarnated. We were all under the assumption the line had died out."

"Well, it didn't," Jae said, moving closer to them. "And I know this because the Lotus empress... is my sister."

Mayhara's jaw dropped slightly. "What? No." She didn't know why she'd blatantly called it out as if implying he was lying, but her mind couldn't process what he'd said. "How old is your sister?"

"She just turned eighteen."

"What?" Mayhara scoffed. "You want me to believe the Lotus empress has been alive for eighteen years and nobody knew about her?"

"Not exactly. Few knew——"

Mayhara cut him off as she pushed back her hair from her temples, her mind full of confusion. "But... But if your sister is the empress, and she's around our age, she would have been at school with us."

"When my parents found out about her, they feared for her life. They told no one. They hid the truth and kept her safe at home. They felt she was at risk because of the rumors about the Pishacha."

Mayhara's brow furrowed as she tried to remember how the legend went.

Darshana was the one to remind her. "Upon the one

hundredth reincarnation of the Lotus empress, the dark god Kashmeru would send out his shadow army—Pishacha—to destroy the reborn empress, which in turn would bring about the collapse of the universe."

"So my parents kept her hidden," Jae said.

"But that's just an old made-up tale." Mayhara almost laughed. "Something we were told as children to scare us."

"It doesn't feel like a false threat when the possibility of a family member being killed hovers over you. Not to mention the world being destroyed. My parents didn't want to take any chances."

"And now they're looking for her," Mayhara guessed. "The Pishacha. They somehow found out."

"You could say that," Jae said, letting out a sigh. "Except it's a little more complicated."

"Complicated how?"

"Naree—my sister," Jae explained, "has been encumbered by the dark spirit of Kashmeru."

Mayhara blinked. "What do you mean? She's... possessed?"

"Not exactly." Jae seemed as if he were struggling to find the words.

Darshana spoke up. "Kashmeru has sent his spirit

messenger, Bhutano, to collect her. Through Bhutano, Kashmeru's spirit is speaking into Naree's mind, seeking out the thousand-year-old soul of Lakshmi, the Lotus empress. He calls her to his tomb."

Mayhara shook her head. "Why?"

"He needs her blood," Jae said. "According to the legend, the empress's blood is needed to release the spell that keeps the whole of his spirit trapped in its tomb."

"If Kashmeru is successful in calling her to his tomb," Darshana said, "he will be born again and bring about the collapse of the universe."

"His messenger, Bhutano, is traveling in the body of a human he has possessed." Jae took a step forward. "He's taken her. And we have to track him down."

"She's been kidnapped?" Mayhara asked.

"You could say that. But it would appear she's gone with him willingly." Jae let out an indignant sigh, frustrated with the story himself. "Lakshmi's spirit dwells within Naree, and the connection Lakshmi has to Kashmeru is one of the most powerful bonds in history. Naree cannot help it—Lakshmi is drawn to him when she's called. It's as if she's under a spell."

"But I thought Lakshmi hated Kashmeru," Mayhara

said.

"Yes and no." Darshana locked her hands behind her back and began to pace. "Kashmeru is Lakshmi's greatest love. And vice versa. They are, indeed, soul mates. But the evil and darkness that exists in Kashmeru's soul keeps them from being together. Lakshmi is pure light, pure and good energy, and that energy clashes with the darkness within Kashmeru. They cannot exist in the same plane. They each destroy one another. They are of a doomed love."

Mayhara could only stare at Darshana as she struggled to wrap her head around the information. "So Kashmeru is calling the empress to him to take her blood and be reborn."

"In order to destroy the world." Darshana nodded. "Yes."

"And you think that somehow I can help stop this?" Mayhara shook her head again. "Why? Why me?"

"Bhutano is very powerful," Darshana said. "There is no doubt he is collecting the Pishacha army to ensure the empress's journey to Kashmeru's tomb. A gathering of the elite mages is needed in order to stop them."

"But I'm not… I wasn't the top of my class."

"No." Darshana pressed her lips into a tight line for a moment. "But you are the most elite crimson mage who remains alive."

Mayhara blanched. "What? What happened to Fei Ling?"

Darshana lowered her head. "She was found dead just last week."

"No." Mayhara felt as if her heart stopped. Fei Ling had been her idol. She'd always worked hard to match the skill of Fei Ling's crimson mage energy. She put a hand on her chest, feeling the sad rhythm of her heart. "How did she die?"

"They think it was murder," Jae said. "But we haven't heard anything about the investigation going any further. It seems to have been buried behind other stories."

"Buried?"

"By the government, probably. They shut down our school without anyone blinking an eye. It shouldn't surprise you that they've got their hands in every business and organization in New United Asia, including the media."

Mayhara thought back on how their school had been shut down, how any pushback regarding the wait for the reincarnated Lotus empress had been quickly nipped in the bud. The public outcry had been swiftly silenced by arrests and new laws against mages. It was almost as if the government had taken their shot at being the greatest power in the land before anyone could stop them.

"What happened after the Eradication?" Mayhara asked. "What happened to the others? I lost track of everyone. And then I had no way of finding out."

"Most of the mages and their families were taken to prison camps, as I'm sure you know. Though some did as you did and gave in to the order."

"I don't see how it's much different," Jae said. "Being constantly monitored, forbidden from using your powers, told what to do and how to live … it's practically the same as being imprisoned."

"But I have a chance to get my family out," Mayhara said as a burning feeling covered the back of her neck. "It may take years, but I can get them out of there."

"Out of one prison and into another," Jae mumbled.

Aggravation tore at her. "What do you want from me? How do you expect me to help?"

Darshana wrinkled her brow and reached out, grabbing Mayhara by the wrist. She lifted her jacket sleeve and scowled. "Where's your wristband?"

Mayhara blinked. She had forgotten about her garnet stone wristband. All mages wore leather wristbands with corresponding stones that amplified their powers. Each stone was cleansed by a guru, cleared of all negative energy and made ready to be used for the purpose of helping in the protection of the Lotus empress. Because Mayhara wasn't allowed to use her power, she'd stopped wearing it. It was tucked away in a box in her apartment. The government didn't know about the wristbands, apparently, because they'd never demanded it from her.

"It's at my place," Mayhara said. "Why?"

"You're going to need it if you're going to be any help at all. We're going to need all the power we can harness. If there ever was a time to make sure you're wearing it, it's now."

Mayhara glanced at Jae, noticing his wristband. A sapphire stone caught the light, and she remembered he was a sapphire mage.

"I still don't understand how I'm supposed to help."

Darshana placed a gentle hand on her shoulder. "You know the prophecy of the legend?"

"I think so." Mayhara's brow wrinkled. "The Council

of the Seven—the leading dark mages of the Pishacha. They want the blood of the Lotus empress to release Kashmeru."

"And you need to help stop that from happening," Darshana said.

"We need to find my sister and keep her from the Seven."

Mayhara's gaze darted between the two. "And that means going against my agreement with the government. That means breaking the law." It would mean her chance of getting her family out of the prison camp would disappear.

"Yes," Darshana said, her eyes locked on Mayhara. "But to save the world, it's our only hope."

Five

Every nerve in Naree's body burned. She wanted to run. But simultaneously, she needed to see Kashmeru. To be with him. It had been too long, and the bond between them had her buzzing with want.

He was like a drug. She knew it was wrong, that it would only lead to peril, but she could not resist him.

She followed the men—his army, the Pishacha—

through the dark streets to the waiting car. She couldn't see their faces clearly because of the black mouth masks they wore. Only the one named Bruno had his face exposed for her to see.

Bruno opened the door for her and gave her a slight nod. She shivered, rubbing at her arms, before climbing into the back seat.

I'm waiting for you, Lakshmi.

She sniffed back her tears. "This is wrong," she whispered.

Come to me. You feel it in your heart. We need to be together.

The core of her body stirred. A hot, pulsing urge, centuries in the making. "I'm afraid," she said.

All will be as it should, my love.

Her skin prickled with ice. "No. I know what's inside you. Your vision of what should be is full of pain and sorrow. I cannot give myself to you."

Yet she was frozen in place. Unable to move. Unable to run.

Kashmeru beckoned, and it was fate that Lakshmi would answer.

Six

Mayhara hardly noticed anything during the train ride home. Her mind was ablur with everything she had just learned, and her chest felt heavy with the seriousness of the situation. Though her gaze touched upon the moonlit landscape, questions about the Lotus empress saturated her thoughts.

As did the unexpected news of Fei Ling's death.

She couldn't wrap her head around it. Fei Ling was someone she'd admired. Her skills in crimson power had been unparalleled compared to anyone else's in their school. And now she was dead. Murdered. All in some large-scheme plot to stop the empire from resurfacing.

She needed to calm down. She squeezed her eyes closed for a moment and thought of the mages. There were seven houses back at the academy, one for each type of mage. And each of the seven had a corresponding power. The mages were born with their specific power, and the academy's purpose had been to help them learn to control those powers.

Mayhara touched her bare wrist, thinking about her garnet wristband and remembering the houses.

Crimson mages: earth, stability, survival, security.
Copper mages: water, ice, pleasure, guilt.
Golden mages: fire, willpower, shame.
Emerald mages: air, wind, heart, love, grief.
Sapphire mages: throat, sound, truth, lies.
Amethyst mages: vision, sight, illusions, secrets.
Diamond mages: spirituality, emotion, virtue, integrity.

And the Lotus had all these powers. Every single one. Which made her both powerful and a target.

When she stepped off the train, her eyes went to the

sky. Her gaze landed on the hazy streak that faintly smudged the panorama of stars. The Akutake comet was approaching. The newscasters had been mentioning it for over a year now. The celestial event was connected to the legend of Kashmeru and Lakshmi, but before knowing that the Lotus had been reborn, Mayhara hadn't paid much attention to it. Now, knowing the truth, Mayhara's skin grew icy cold. It was all falling into place, whether she was ready or not. With a shiver, she pulled her hood tighter over her head.

Before she knew it, she'd reached her apartment complex. It was quiet. Too quiet. Of course, it all could have been in Mayhara's mind. After all, one of the biggest lies she'd been led to believe had just been unraveled before her eyes.

The Lotus empress had been reborn, and she needed Mayhara's help.

When the elevator doors opened on her floor, the faint sound of her neighbor's televiewer gave her a sense of normalcy. Though she felt her world had been tipped on its head, it instilled a fraction of calm to know some things were still the same.

She reached her door and tapped her keycode into the

lock pad. It beeped twice. Mayhara frowned. Normally, it would beep once, the lock light would switch from red to green, and her door would click open.

But the lock light remained red.

She rolled her eyes. She'd probably been so caught up in the events of the night that she'd punched in the wrong code.

She tapped the code in again, this time slowly, deliberately pressing each number of the code to be sure she didn't make a mistake. The device beeped once, and the light turned green. Mayhara let out a soft sigh of relief as the door clicked open.

She stepped inside, ready to remove her jacket, but she stopped short when her apartment lights didn't switch on. What was going on? First the lock pad and then the lights. *Probably a glitch in the electrical system*, she thought.

Resolving to do things the old-fashioned way, Mayhara felt for the wall near the front door, searching for the manual control panel. With a touch of her fingertip, the control panel lit up. She swiped the menu to the light settings and pressed the symbol for the living room. She squinted as the room lit up.

But when she turned around, she clapped a hand over

her mouth and let a scream erupt into it.

Her heart leaped into a rhythm her mind couldn't keep up with.

Crumpled on the floor with a bullet wound in her head was Riya. The dress she had wanted to borrow sat in a wrinkled lump beside her. Riya's lifeless eyes were rolled back in her head, and her mouth was agape. Mayhara imagined the scream that was lost to the room—only to be heard by whoever had murdered her.

With a shuddered breath, Mayhara slowly moved closer to Riya's body. Her eyes shot back and forth between the puddle of blood where Riya's head rested and the rest of the room. Was she alone? Or had the killer remained behind to add Mayhara to their list of victims?

Barely able to breathe, she reached out to touch Riya's arm. Before she could even make contact, her eyes filled with tears and her skin crawled in fear.

Who did this? And why?

She wished mage power could heal. But maybe even healing wouldn't bring someone back to life. Wiping the tears from her cheeks, her mind raced with what she should do. Should she stay with Riya's body, or leave the apartment to call the police? As she struggled with the dilemma, a flash of something black and rectangular caught her eye. Without thinking, she reached for it. It was a plastic card, like a credit card, but there were no words or numbers on it. The only thing of significance on it was a thin horizontal line with a crescent moon on the upper right side. She flipped it over to find a computer chip. Was this Riya's, or had someone left it behind?

Mayhara stood and pulled out her Linq. She wasn't up for a visit from the authorities, but she had to report finding Riya's body.

As she swiped on her Linq, she heard a thump in her bedroom. Shockwaves of fear burst inside of her, causing her to back away from the sound. The back of her leg hit something—Riya's oversized bag, she realized. The collision caused her to stumble backward. Landing on her tailbone, she let out a muffled curse as her Linq and the mysterious card she found flew from her grasp.

Before she could retrieve her Linq, a figure moved from the darkness of her bedroom into the dim light of the living room. He was masked, dressed in black, and he moved toward Mayhara with a violent gait.

She scrambled to her feet, hardly able to catch her breath. Without thinking, she grabbed the lamp on the end table next to the couch and hurled it at the masked man. He blocked it with his arm, but it slowed him down.

Mayhara dove for her Linq, but the man pounced on her, grabbing her by the waist and twisting her away from the device. She screamed as her fingers dug into his hands in an attempt to pry him off of her. One of his hands loosened, but it was quickly repositioned onto the back of her neck. With a squeeze, the man sent Mayhara careening into the wall.

Black spots danced in her vision. Head spinning, Mayhara forced herself upright. Though she knew it would hurt, she called upon her mage powers and held her palms toward the man. Crimson particles formulated at the surface of her hands, and she quickly hurled a blast of crimson energy at the man. One ball of crimson caught him in the chest, pitching him back until he tripped over her coffee table. Mayhara shifted forward, ready to shoot another blast of crimson his way, but the man resurfaced with a shiny object in his hands.

Her breath stuck in her throat as she realized it was a taser pistol.

He fired the gun.

She tried to block the electrified bullet with her

crimson particles, but the bullet was too fast. A searing pain cut across the outer side of her arm, causing her to cry out in agony. Her hand clasped over her wound, immediately slick with blood. But she couldn't feel the slug bullet, and there was an absence of electric shock— the bullet must have just grazed her.

The masked man had the barrel of the gun aimed at her as he stomped forward.

Mayhara couldn't breathe, backing up as if it would prevent the man from reaching her. Just then, a beep sounded, and the front door burst open. As two police officers barged into her apartment with weapons drawn, the masked man stopped in his tracks.

One moment, Mayhara was lifting her arms to show the police she was unarmed, and the next moment, she turned her head to find the masked man had disappeared.

The closer of the two officers aimed her gun at Mayhara, her eyes quickly darting to the unmoving form of Riya sprawled out on the floor. "Don't move."

Though the pain from her wound was intense, Mayhara kept her arms up. "This is my apartment."

The second officer crouched down to inspect Riya. He placed two fingers on her neck. After a moment he let out a disheartened grunt, and then he pulled out a monitoring device and held it over her heart. He looked up at his fellow officer and shook his head. "She's dead."

The female officer set her mouth in a straight line and took a step closer to Mayhara. "Miss, put your hands behind your head and turn around."

"But I… but I found her like this. There's someone else here. He's broken in and attacked me."

Her hands were pulled down and drawn together. The next thing Mayhara felt was the cold steel of electro-cuffs locking onto her wrists.

"Wait. No. I didn't kill her," she pleaded.

"Save it, miss," the officer said. "You're under arrest."

Seven

Naree watched from the back of the parked car as Bruno met with a hooded man in the back alleyway. She couldn't hear their conversation, but she didn't miss the brown-paper bundle the hooded man handed Bruno. Bruno held out his Linq, as did the hooded man. Naree could almost make out the faint beeping of their devices as credits were transferred from Bruno's device to that of the hooded man's.

Bruno tucked the small package inside his trench coat and waited as the hooded man ducked his head and walked away into the night. When Bruno brought his Linq up to his ear, Naree used her powers to listen more clearly to what he was saying.

"Yes, Bhutano," Bruno said. "I've got it. Yes, she's still secure. I'll await further instructions."

Naree let out a shuddered breath and leaned back in her seat as Bruno came back to the car.

"What's in the package?" Naree asked once he was inside.

"You'll see soon enough."

His words weren't harsh, but they angered Naree. She knew this was part of the prophecy. Something that she must have lived through before, in her other lives, but she couldn't remember it all. Only bits and traces.

As they drove, she gazed out the window, her eyes finding the faint streak in the sky that played a part in her destiny.

She balled her hands into fists, frustrated with her fate, irritated with the magnetic pull Kashmeru had on her. Pissed at herself that she couldn't fight it.

She didn't want the prophecy to be fulfilled. She

didn't want to be the reason the universe collapsed. If only she could figure out how to resist him.

Eight

A loud bang thundering in her ears, Mayhara rolled hard against the side of the transport. She blinked, forcing herself to wake up from the electric-pulse-induced sleep the police had put her into. Her memory came back to her; she'd tried to get away as they'd dragged her out of her apartment, so they'd knocked her out with an electro-pulse to the neck. But she couldn't have been out long. She didn't live that far away from the station, and she was still in the transport.

She needed to move her hair out of her face, but her wrists were still cuffed behind her back. It took her a moment to adjust her position on the bench in the back of the van and focus her attention out the window.

City lights were scattered around them. They were downtown now. Close to the station.

The officer in the passenger seat turned his head and glared back at her through the laser-screen divider. "She's awake."

"Good," the driver—the female officer who'd cuffed her—said, sparing her a glance in the rearview mirror. "Didn't really feel like carrying her into the station."

Mayhara's throat felt dry. Her body still ached from the attack in her apartment, but she had to push her pain aside and concentrate on what she was going to say. They thought she'd killed Riya. She could only hope they'd believe her when she proclaimed her innocence.

"CL17 to base," the driver said aloud.

Something on the dashboard beeped. "This is base. Go ahead, CL17."

"10-19 with suspect in custody. We'll be up in a minute."

Outside the transporter windows, everything went dark. It took Mayhara a moment to realize they'd entered the parking garage under the police station.

She was jostled forward as the van came to a sudden stop. The transporter let out a ping as the engine shut off, and the officers exited the vehicle. Mayhara listened as their footsteps crunched along the gritty surface of the parking lot, and then a loud double beep alerted her that the back doors were about to open.

The female officer narrowed her eyes at her. Mayhara knew she was speculating whether or not she was going to give them a hard time. She decided to cooperate. It wouldn't help her case to put up a fight, innocent or not.

After scooting toward the door, the female officer took her by the arm to help her out of the van. With a firm grip, she led Mayhara away from the van as the other officer slammed the doors shut. The parking garage was full of police vans, and an elevator entrance could be seen at the far end of the garage.

As they made their way to the elevator, Mayhara tried to steady her breath. She wasn't sure if they would hook her up to a lie detector, but if her heart was racing, anything she said would be construed as a lie. She would have to calm down, and fast.

But calming down after finding her friend murdered in her apartment was impossible. *Poor Riya.* She had only wanted to borrow a dress. To go out with the guy she'd been pining over and maybe start a new chapter of her life. And now she was dead.

Who was the masked man, and had he killed Riya thinking she was Mayhara?

Mayhara swallowed hard, suddenly realizing that she had probably been the target. The news of Fei Ling's death came back to her.

You are the most elite crimson mage who remains alive, Darshana had said. Which meant it was most likely the Pishacha who'd killed Riya. The Pishacha were out to kill Mayhara.

I'm the elite crimson mage now, she thought. *I'm a target.*

She squinted against the bright, halogen lights of the station as they entered the building. As they passed through a maze of hallways, other officers of the Imperial Police cast her glances. She wanted to scream at all of them that she was innocent. That she was the target of a murderer. That there were real bad guys out there actually killing people, and the police should be dragging *them* in instead.

The female officer tugged on her arm as they stopped in front of a windowed door. The male officer opened it for them, and Mayhara was brought to a chair on one side of a black table. Her cuffs were unlocked, and the female officer glared at her a look as if daring her to make a run for it. Mayhara rubbed at her wrists and squirmed in her chair but remained where she was.

The male officer was the first to leave the room. Mayhara kept her eyes on the female officer, who was obviously convinced Mayhara was guilty.

"Sit tight," the officer said. "Our interrogation officer will be in shortly to talk with you. Until then, don't even think about going near that door."

Mayhara nodded sheepishly, her head swimming with how she was going to explain herself.

As the door shut behind the officer, Mayhara squeezed her eyes shut and raked her hands through her hair. What was she going to do? She wouldn't be able to explain her whereabouts before she'd come home to the apartment. If she told the Imperial police about the Lotus princess and her potential involvement, they'd probably send her off to a prison camp. No, she was going to have to be strategic in her answers without making it appear as if she was guilty of Riya's murder.

She took in the sight of the enormous mirror across from her. No doubt it was two-way glass with officers on the other side studying her. She wiped at her cheeks and kept her eyes on the table, practicing her guru's breathing techniques.

The door clicked open, and despite her determination to stay calm, Mayhara's heart hammered in her chest, and sweat formed at her temples.

"Good evening, Miss Guatama. I'm Chief Inspector Khapoor. I'm sure you know why we brought you in."

"My bets are on the dead body in my apartment." She flinched as soon as she said it, realizing how awful it sounded. Her adrenaline must have been doing a number on her attitude.

"Yes," Khapoor said, studying her face as he sat across from her. "Is there anything you'd like to say about that?"

"I didn't kill her. I swear. Riya is—was—my friend. I came home and found her there."

"Came home from where? And can anyone confirm your whereabouts?"

She kept a straight face. "I went for a walk. And no, no one saw me, and I didn't talk to anyone, so no one can confirm it, but I'm sure you can estimate the time of death and check the apartment building computer system for what time I came home."

"And how exactly did the victim get into your apartment before you?"

"I gave her my key code."

"Allegedly. We can ask the apartment manager to check the video feed from the hall." He glanced back at the big mirror and nodded, no doubt signaling for whoever was behind it to get the video feed. "But you could have entered the apartment with her, and following that theory, killed her. Then you could have left your apartment to use your key code and come back in, thinking it would throw off the investigation."

Her jaw dropped. "No. No, I found her there, dead on my floor. And she wasn't alone. There was someone else in the apartment. He came out of the bedroom and attacked me."

Khapoor took out a small notepad from his shirt pocket and flipped it open. He clicked open a pen and began jotting down notes. "I see. Can you describe this person?"

"He was masked, but about a half a head taller than me. I'm sorry. I didn't have much time to analyze him; he attacked me."

Khapoor continued writing. "And where was this perpetrator when our officers arrived?"

"I… I don't know. He disappeared."

Khapoor stopped writing and looked up at her. "Disappeared?"

"Y-Yes. One minute he was there, and the next minute he was gone."

Khapoor put down his pen and pinched the bridge of his nose. "Miss Guatama, are you currently under the influence of alcohol or drugs?"

"No. No, I'm not. Listen, I know it sounds crazy, but there was a man in my apartment. He attacked me. Look at my arm. He shot me with a taser-pistol. I'm sure he's the one who killed Riya."

With one raised bushy eyebrow, Khapoor took a two-second glance at the torn and singed material of Mayhara's sleeve.

"If someone shot a taser-pistol, there would be evidence of it in your apartment. A shell or a burn mark, if not the bullet itself—assuming it didn't penetrate you. It if did, it's a miracle you aren't in the hospital now instead of sitting here in interrogation."

A small ray of hope sparked in Mayhara's chest. "Yes, evidence. There must be something."

Khapoor closed his notebook and returned it to his pocket. "I'm sure you're not opposed to waiting here while we check out your story?"

Mayhara nodded. "Yeah, I'll wait."

"Did you want us to call anyone? A lawyer?"

She studied his face, wondering if the government would assign someone to her case who wouldn't really be on her side. All the lawyers were working for government. They had nothing to gain by taking her side. "No." Mayhara shook her head. "No one."

Chief Inspector Khapoor stood and gave Mayhara a solitary nod of his head before leaving the room. All Mayhara could do now was wait. Surely the officers would find a burn mark or the shell from the taser-bullet. Surely the video surveillance would show someone going into her apartment besides Riya before Mayhara had gotten back.

A shiver suddenly crept along Mayhara's skin. Her spark of hope was all at once extinguished into a puff of smoke. If the masked man could disappear without a trace, if he'd managed to leave her apartment without anyone seeing him, then it would be totally feasible that he could have gotten into her apartment without being detected as well. She wasn't being paranoid. This was real. And it scared her to the core.

Nine

They must have known the owners, Naree thought. Or the owners were also Pishacha. The other tables at the restaurant were unoccupied. They'd closed down the place for them so they could do this privately.

Bruno sat across from Naree, the journal he'd unwrapped from the brown-paper parcel lying between them, opened to a page scribbled with ancient ink. One of Bruno's men leaned forward on the table, playing with a pair of chopsticks.

"Anything?" Bruno asked.

Naree shook her head. She'd been staring at the sketch of a dagger on the withered page for almost an hour. Bruno had said she might get some insight from the drawing. Something that would help their mission.

But nothing came.

She didn't know whether to expect the memories of her last lives to come back to her all at once. But Bruno was convinced that the clues were there, lurking near the surface. He'd said Kashmeru had told him so. He'd said that Kashmeru promised him salvation if he helped his plight.

The bell above the door rang as one of Bruno's men entered. Bruno stood and buttoned his blazer, stepping out of their booth as the man approached.

"Did you take care of her?" Bruno asked in a low voice.

The man nodded and whispered something back to him. Naree wanted to use her powers to hear them better, but she knew it would upset Bruno. And Kashmeru. He was also watching and listening, after all.

Bruno's Linq chirped. He studied it for a moment, his brow raised. Reaching over the table, he closed the journal and grabbed his trench coat from his chair.

"We've got something," he said. "Come on. We need to go."

"Where are we going?" Naree asked.

"One of my guys found a lead. We need to go meet him and check it out. Maybe it will help spark some memory."

Naree tucked a strand of hair behind her ear. "It's late."

The corner of Bruno's mouth crept upward for a split second. "The end of the world is upon us, Your Highness. We haven't got a moment to spare."

Ten

It took all her meditation training and control techniques to not panic. Everything she had an impulse to do—bouncing her leg, biting her nails, folding her hands together—she decided against. She was paranoid that anything she did could be construed as guilty body language. Then again, remaining abnormally calm could be construed as suspicious, too. Not that it ultimately mattered. She had a feeling if the government or the Pishacha wanted to frame her, then that was exactly what they'd accomplish.

There was no clock in the interrogation room, so Mayhara could only assume she'd been waiting an hour before Chief Inspector Khapoor finally returned. His eyes met with Mayhara's for a moment before he cleared his throat and took the seat across from her.

Mayhara scooted forward in her chair, hoping he had something good to tell her.

"Miss Guatama, thank you for your patience," he said, but Mayhara could already tell from his tone that things were not going to go her way. "We had some officers check your apartment, as well as collect the video footage from the hall of your apartment building."

She held her breath.

"There was no sign of a taser-pistol being fired in your apartment. There were also no signs of a break in. The surveillance videos show your friend Riya entering your apartment at approximately 5:35 P.M. and you entering the apartment just ten minutes later."

"What? No. No, that's impossible." She felt as if a vise squeezed her heart and lungs and ribs. She could barely catch her breath. "I didn't get home until much later. It was at least 8 o'clock, probably later." Mayhara considered looking for her sub-train ticket to confirm the time, but then the officers would know about her traveling to the school. But maybe that would be the better option. Being charged with mage-related crimes would be better than being accused of murder, wouldn't it?

No. It didn't matter. She was obviously being set up. The video footage had been tampered with. Someone had forged the times on the recordings to make it look like she had been home earlier.

"What about the lock pad?" she asked in desperation.

Khapoor let out a sigh. "The computer monitoring system shows there were only two instances of your apartment door being opened. One at 5:35, and one at 5:45."

That's impossible.

Mayhara felt numb. She wasn't sure who had done it—the police, the government, the Pishacha—but whoever it was, she was being framed.

Her body began to shake. She squeezed her palms shut, trying to regain control.

"Miss Guatama, I'm afraid we're going to have to put you in a holding cell until we can officially transfer you to a prison camp."

"What? But don't I get a trial or something? Don't I get a chance to prove my innocence?"

"You can petition to have a trial and seek out council, but I have to warn you: nowadays, that can take months. It won't be denied to you, however. You just have to fill out the forms."

Mayhara was frozen. She wasn't sure if this was really happening or if she was suffering from a nightmare. All she had worked for, everything she had sacrificed, it all meant nothing. All of it, gone in one night. There would be no chance for her to save her family. And it would be too much to believe she would be joining them at the same camp. No. The government would ensure they would stay separated. She knew how the system worked.

"Miss Guatama," Khapoor said as he checked his watch. "I'm going to ask you to come with me now. There are two armed officers right outside this door who are going to escort you to the processing center. I do hope you will cooperate, so this can all go smoothly without any problems. We don't anticipate any problems, do we?"

Mayhara understood that the man was tired and didn't want her to put up a fight. Though Mayhara was just as exhausted, her body was hopped up on adrenaline. And fear.

She shook her head anyway.

Joining Khapoor in the hall, Mayhara felt as if she were walking in someone else's reality. She walked along in a trance, her eyes set on the back of the officer in front of her, the sounds reaching her ears muffled and the things she passed in the halls blurred.

In a daze, she followed the officer's instructions to place her hand on the info-tablet to record her fingerprints and access her data. She was then led to a holding cell at the back of the building until they could process her and move her to a prison camp. The officer said she should settle in for the night since the next transport wouldn't be until morning. Though she faced him, her gaze went right through him as he explained that the cell was electronically monitored and could detect if someone tried to tamper with the lock. She barely realized she nodded at him as she dropped her weight onto the bench against the wall.

At least she was alone. There was no one there to bother her, no one to ask her why she was there. No one to ask her questions she didn't really feel like answering.

What should I do? she thought. *Should I call someone?*

She didn't have her Linq. It had been lost in the scuffle at her apartment, and there was no telling if the police had seized it or not. If only there was a way to call Darshana without the police knowing who she was calling. If only someone out there was on her side.

Leaning her head back against the wall, she scolded herself for despairing so much. She brought to mind the positivity training Darshana had taught her.

She leaned her head back against the wall and tried to clear her mind. She had to call upon a happy thought. Even in this time of desperation, she had to find something that might bring her joy. She could hear voices in the distance, officers chatting with each other, doors being opened and closed with an electronic beep, the shuffling of feet. Squeezing her eyes shut, she tried to block it all out.

What do I have to be happy about? There must be something. As dire as things are…

Then a face came into her mind. Just this morning, on her way to work, a little girl had dropped her school books. Papers flew everywhere, scattered by the wind. Mayhara had been in a hurry, but she had stopped anyway. She'd helped the little girl until everything she'd lost had been put back into her hands. And the little girl had smiled at Mayhara, a big, grateful, gap-toothed smile, and she'd said thank you and told Mayhara that she was nice.

Mayhara opened her eyes and smiled at the memory.

A figure came around the corner and into the holding cell area. His police uniform was pressed, and his buttons were shiny, but he kept his head down. He glanced over his shoulder, then approached the bars of the cell.

When he lifted his head, Mayhara gasped.

Jae lifted a finger to his lips to silence her as he pulled out his Linq from his pocket.

With a shuddered breath, Mayhara jumped from the bench and hurried to the bars. "What are you doing?" she whispered.

"Getting you out of here. Or did you pay for the weekend package?"

"It won't work. The whole cell is electronically monitored. I don't think you can even touch the bars without setting off some kind of sensor."

He huffed a quick laugh and attached a wire from his Linq into some port in the lock.

She narrowed her eyes, watching what he was doing.

"You're a hacker."

"I prefer tech prodigy."

She scoffed.

"Who do you think talked Darshana into using a Linq?" he asked.

Something pricked her ears. "Someone's coming."

His device beeped quietly, and the cell doors slid open.

"Hurry," Jae said, grabbing her hand.

Instead of going the way he'd come in, they went farther down the hall, past the other cells.

"Do you know where you're going?" Mayhara asked.

Jae pulled out his Linq, checking the screen. A small glowing blue line showed a route through the building. "Just need to hack through a door or two."

Mayhara checked over her shoulder as they ran, cringing any time they had to stop so Jae could manipulate a locked door. If she hadn't been so anxious about getting caught, she might have been able to admire his smooth technique and clever know-how.

He brought her to a stairwell and began descending. "Just one floor to the exit, and we'll be out of the building," he said.

Her chest filled with hope. They might actually make it. Sure, she would be on the run. There was no way she could go back to work. The police and the Pishacha would be after her, and she would constantly be in fear of getting caught. But knowing she was one doorway away from escaping filled her with exhilaration.

Jae cracked the code for the final door and pulled her through it.

Suddenly, red lights flashed and an alarm sounded. Mayhara reached for her neck, a buzzing shock pricking the skin where her blocker was embedded.

Jae hardened his jaw and shook his head, pulling her along. "We're going to need to get that thing out of your neck. It's only a matter of time before they track you down. Come on."

He dragged her to a motorcycle and climbed on. She jumped behind him without so much as a question about a helmet. With chaos exploding around them, they raced out of the lot and into the cold chill of the night.

Eleven

Naree leaned over the sink and stared at her reflection. The bathroom was private. Sure, the Pishacha stood guard outside, waiting for her to come out, but no one would be coming in. For a moment, she had a reprieve.

Lakshmi, I long to hold you again.

Naree swiped the back of her hand over her forehead,

which was moist with sweat. Kashmeru's hold was getting stronger, and it was getting harder to resist his call. Any resistance was met with feverish chills, nausea, and a churning in the pit of her stomach. Though part of her still desired to flee, a deeper part of her, the core of her, was desperate to be with Kashmeru again.

Please come to me, my love.

"I'm doing everything you ask of me." Her voice was strained, hoarse with the threat of sobs.

Remember how good it feels to be together. Remember it, my love.

Naree felt a tightness in her chest. She squeezed her eyes shut, and visions filled her head.

Kashmeru stood before her in a courtyard. She could see a temple behind him, the white marble seeming to reach the skies. He was tall and handsome, and his golden-brown eyes twinkled as he held her gaze. He held out a hand, and she placed hers in it. His touch was electrifying. A shiver pulsed through her as he pulled her closer.

He leaned closer to her ear. The warm caress of his breath as he pledged his love made her gasp in pleasure. He kissed her neck, and she pressed herself into his chest. Everything else ceased to exist. It was just the two of them.

Kashmeru and Lakshmi. They could live forever in each other's arms, without need for anything or anyone else.

She looked up at him, their eyes locking as she was about to accept his kiss.

But his eyes grew black. As dark as death.

She pulled away.

Naree opened her eyes, a stifled cry escaping her lips.

No, my love. It can be perfect between us if you just let me in.

She reached for her neck, the feel of his gentle lips lingering there as if it hadn't been almost a century ago. "I don't know if I can."

It is our destiny, Lakshmi. You cannot deny it. We belong together.

Twelve

Wincing, Mayhara gingerly patted the gauzy patch on her neck.

"Don't mess with that too much," Jae said. "It won't completely erase the signal. It'll just throw them off. Blurs your location. They could eventually track you down if they get close enough."

"Sorry." Mayhara sheepishly put her hand down and slipped it between her knees. "Just stings like a bitch." She sat on the edge of an out-of-commission fountain at the academy.

Jae shot her a quick smirk before checking his Linq. He pressed his lips into a tight line and then tucked the device away. Mayhara knew he was trying not to show how frustrated he was, but she could feel it. She was just as frustrated. They had sent Darshana a message over an hour ago but still hadn't gotten a response.

"Do you really think it's safe here?" she asked.

He shrugged with one shoulder. "We're going to have to take our chances until we figure out what to do. But for now, it's probably the safest place in New India." He checked his Linq again. "Where is she?"

"I hope she's all right. Maybe she heard about the prison break and is keeping a low profile in case someone tries to follow her."

Jae nodded. "Yeah, makes sense. She's escaped them before, when they tried to arrest her after the Eradication. Well, if she doesn't write back in the next hour, we'll have to head out. Isn't safe to stay in one place, especially with that thing in your neck."

He walked toward her, his eyes on her neck, and Mayhara swore she could see the wheels turning in his mind from the look on his face.

"I can do it, you know," he said.

"What? Take it out? Did you go and get your medical degree in the last two years?"

"No, but my aunt is a vet."

"Um, occupation experience isn't linked via blood, you know? And, uh, I'm not exactly a dog."

"I spent a lot of time with her, stayed with her one summer. I hung around when she'd fix up the animals and stuff. I'm not saying I could perform organ surgery, but I'm pretty sure I'm adept enough to remove your blocker without hitting any major arteries."

Instinctively, Mayhara placed a hand over the patch.

A small laugh drifted from his lips. "I think you're just going to have to trust me. I've got some supplies at my apartment, though I'm a little leery about the police or the Pishacha tracking us down there."

She sat up a little straighter. "What about the nursing facilities?"

He narrowed his eyes and nodded slowly.

"I don't know what damage has been done to it," she said, "but I'm sure they couldn't have destroyed everything."

"It's worth a look. Let's go."

They headed for the East Quarter building where the nursing facilities had been located. Mayhara held on to the hope that the facilities hadn't been destroyed altogether. Not that she was looking forward to Jae cutting into her neck, but if there was a chance to throw the police off their scent, she knew they had to take it.

As she walked beside him, she noticed how square he kept his shoulders, how raised he kept his chin, and how his intense eyes seemed to take in everything in his sights. She felt as if he did more than just look at things; he really *saw* everything and understood what was there.

He gave her a sideward glance. "What?"

Ignoring the spread of heat to her cheeks, she asked, "So you didn't go back to Korea when the school closed?"

"I did. I wanted to help keep Naree safe, but our father started noticing strange things in our hometown. Like strangers lurking about and people asking questions. He told me to take her somewhere else, somewhere no one would suspect."

"You brought her to New India? Didn't you think that was like bringing the lamb to the lion's den?"

"Hide in plain sight. That's what they say."

They turned down the corridor, getting closer to the nursing facilities.

"Things were fine for a while, but then Naree started changing. She was acting like someone else and doing strange things. She kept disappearing, sneaking out at night. I decided to follow her and found out she was meeting up with some guy. I didn't recognize him, but I could tell he was bad news.

"I confronted her, told her she should be careful, but she told me I didn't understand. She would get a strange look on her face, as if she'd become someone I didn't recognize. She told me it was out of her control—it was fate.

"I didn't know what to do. Not only because I have this instinct to protect my little sister, but also because she's the Lotus empress. I mean, I can't just let the ruler of the Lotus empire go rogue into a dangerous city.

"I got worried. I called my parents to let them know my concerns, but she must have overheard me. She was gone the next day." He stopped in the hall. "We're here."

Mayhara watched as he opened the door to the nursing facilities, but her mind was fixated on everything he'd told her. She couldn't imagine not being able to control her own actions, to be drawn to a force so strong she couldn't resist it.

As they stepped into the room, the far-off sounds of sirens grew louder. It was probably instinct, but they both backed against the wall near the door, ears perked and bodies unmoving. Jae was so close, Mayhara breathed him in. She noted something minty in the soap he must have used, and something else—sandalwood?

His head was turned away from her, but his chest was practically pressed up to hers. As the sirens passed, he turned his face toward her, their eyes locking. It took a moment before Mayhara broke the trance and dropped her gaze. Jae cleared his throat and took a step back, swiveling to surveil the room.

Mayhara moved her hair back from her face, hoping her skin would get more cool air to evaporate the sweat that had formed on her temples. The room was only slightly dusty. It didn't appear as though the administration had bothered ransacking the room. It made Mayhara optimistic that they'd be able to find what they needed. As Jae searched a cabinet, Mayhara went toward a set of drawers on the far wall.

She went through two supply-filled drawers before

Jae called out that he'd found a scalpel. In the third drawer, Mayhara found a suture kit.

"You might want to sit somewhere," he said.

Mayhara eyed the examination table and the chair next to the desk in the room. She hopped up on the exam table, figuring it would be better if her neck was closer to eye-level for Jae. Her muscles tensed as he came closer, though she was comforted with the fact that he'd found some disinfectant wipes to clean the scalpel and rub on her neck.

He got as close as he could and lifted his hands near her neck. She moved her hair out of the way and closed her eyes, her fingers grasping the edge of the table.

"Talk about something," she said. "So I don't have to think about this too much."

"Okay." He gently felt her neck, pressing the area, searching for exactly where the blocker was implanted.

She kept her eyes closed, so she wasn't aware of how close the scalpel was until she felt the ice-cold blade on her skin. She sucked in a breath, hoping he would say something more before he actually cut into her.

"When my parents first told me my sister was the Lotus empress, I didn't believe them," he said.

A searing pain stung her neck as he slowly made an incision. Her fingers tightened on the table's edge. "Why not?"

"I thought they just wanted me to be nice to her."

Mayhara almost laughed, but he pushed the blade deeper into her skin, widening the cut.

"I thought it was just a made-up story when I first heard it," she said, forcing her thoughts away from the pain. "A forbidden love between deities. It didn't make sense to me. I thought gods could do whatever they wanted."

"I wouldn't have believed it, either, but seeing the way my sister behaved… It's so unlike her. So either the legend is true, or my sister is under some heavy-duty hypnosis."

Mayhara felt as if he were ripping veins out of her neck. She hoped that wasn't the case. "Why aren't your parents here?"

"They wanted to come. I told them not to. They're not in the best of health, and they've already stressed themselves out to no end getting Naree this far. I promised them I'd take care of it. Not that they didn't argue with me."

The next thing she felt was a needle going through her skin and the sickening slide of thread. She scolded herself for thinking about it. "I wonder where Darshana is."

"That makes two of us."

"I wonder if she's written to my Linq. I dropped it back at my place during the attack. For all I know, it could be in the hands of the police."

"She'd most likely message my device, but we could check it out. We'll have to sneak in and out though. You probably want to pick up a few things anyway. Like your wristband."

"Good idea." She winced as he pressed something sticky upon her neck. "Are you done?"

She heard him chuckle. "You were very brave. I got it out. We're all good."

She cringed as she opened her eyes and took in the sight of bloody cotton on the table beside her. Off to the side was a blood-soaked piece of plastic embedded with tiny computer parts. Jae took a meshy patch, like the one he'd taped to her neck earlier, and wrapped it around the plastic and stuck it in his pocket.

"What do we do with that?" she asked.

"At first I thought we should destroy it, but then I figured we could drop it on a train or something and send the police on a wild goose chase."

Despite herself, she smiled. "I like that idea."

He rested his palms on the table and studied her face. "You okay?"

She resisted touching the bandage on her neck. "Yeah. I'm okay."

He nodded and took out his Linq.

"Anything?" she asked.

"Nope." He tucked it back in his pocket and sighed. "Hey, I want to show you something."

"Okay."

He took her hand to help her off the table. "Follow me."

They headed down a corridor behind the kitchens. Mayhara couldn't remember ever being down this way during her time at the school. She wondered how she could have missed it in all her years at the academy.

"I used to come down here sometimes," he said. "To think and stuff. You know, when everyone else was forming cliques and I was left out."

She gave him a curious look, not remembering him being purposely excluded from any group.

He shrugged. "It wasn't their fault. I guess I mostly kept to myself because of my parents. They were paranoid I'd become close enough friends with someone I'd tell their secret."

They arrived at a staircase that descended into an old stone corridor. He used his Linq to provide light. Pipes ran along the hall, and the farther they went, the more ancient the walls appeared. It was in that moment she realized she trusted Jae enough to let him lead her down some abandoned path under the school.

At the end of the hall was a double door made of withering wood. Instead of a wooden doorframe, it seemed to be surrounded by rock. Jae turned the iron knob on one side of the door and pushed it open. It let out a slow and ominous creak.

"That's not creepy," Mayhara mumbled.

Jae stepped inside, holding his Linq up high so Mayhara could see the room.

No, not a room. A cave.

"What is this?" she asked.

"I don't know. It's always been here. I think the school was built around it. Or, you know, on top of it. Come check this out."

He led her forward. Instead of a floor, there was hard rock and dirt at their feet. The walls and ceiling were all the components of an underground cavern. As they stepped toward the middle of the room, Mayhara noticed that the ground fell away in the center. When Jae repositioned his light, Mayhara could just make out an enormous structure in the center of the cave.

Squinting, she could see the outer surface of some kind of spiral edifice, like a humongous statue made of rock and crystal swirling in a vertical column that reached from the abyss below to the cavern ceiling. It was at least ten feet in diameter.

"What is it?"

"I don't know," Jae said, his voice quiet. "I never asked anyone because I wasn't supposed to be down here. It was different back then: lit up with a glow of swirling particles—I'm assuming mage elements. You can see the seven different sections." He pointed to the curves in the structure. "It was red at the bottom, then orange, yellow, green, blue, purple, and white at the top."

"The mage colors."

"The chakra colors connected to the mages, yes."

She stared at the enormous column in awe. "But it's not lit up anymore."

"I suspect the glow went out when the school shut down."

She paced a bit to the side, trying to see around the structure. "But what is it for?"

"That, I couldn't tell you."

It took a moment before she could tear her eyes away from it. "Do you think it has a significance in Kashmeru calling to Lakshmi?"

He smirked. "You read my mind."

"Maybe Darshana knows."

"I'm sure she'd be the one to ask. If we could just get ahold of her."

Thirteen

The place was crowded, filled with unsuspecting patrons, but Bruno took Naree to a section of the building only a few were allowed to enter. Bruno's man approached and handed him a file.

"Let's sit," Bruno said.

The two of them waited for Naree to take a seat, then joined her. A few of the Pishacha sat as well, and Naree caught a glimpse of their weapons as their leather jackets shifted away from their bodies.

Bruno opened the file so that Naree could see. There was a name and address along with a picture.

"You're sure this is our guy?" Bruno asked his man.

The man nodded. "That's him."

"Have you actually seen the dagger?"

"No," the man said. "But he has to have it."

Bruno studied the picture a moment longer, and then he slid it closer to Naree. "This is him."

Naree swallowed hard as she took in the man's face.

"I don't know if I—"

You must, my love.

Kashmeru's voice had her swallow back her words. Every syllable filled her with longing. His pull on her was growing stronger. It was getting harder and harder for her to fight it. Soon, she would be completely lost to his summoning.

This will bring us one step closer. Soon we will be reunited, and then we can pledge our love to one another, and all will be right in the world.

Fourteen

Though her anxiety was at its peak, Mayhara had to admit it was exhilarating sneaking to the subtrain platform and tossing her blocking device onto one of the trains. Of course, she could only admit this after the fact, when they were far from the scene and in the clear.

With the authorities most likely miles away, she and Jae headed to her apartment to grab her wristband and check if the police had confiscated her Linq. She also wanted to grab a bag of clothes. This would probably be the last time she'd ever be in her apartment, at least until they could rescue Naree, defeat the Pishacha, and prove her innocence.

Instead of going straight to her apartment, Jae had them take a detour to the surveillance room. He quelled Mayhara's fears about getting caught by explaining that nowadays everything was run by automatic settings, that computers, rather than actual people, kept an "eye" on things, lucky for him. It took him no time at all to override the cameras overseeing her hall and disengaging the monitoring of her lock pad.

Aside from worrying about being spotted by neighbors, their venture into her apartment went smoothly. Inside, Mayhara cringed at the state of her once-pristine apartment. She was a minimalist—not one to spend credits on material things while her family was locked away with nothing—but what she did have was strewn about her apartment as if a typhoon had blown through the small space.

At least Riya's body had been taken care of. Mayhara closed her eyes for a moment in reflection of her friend.

She hadn't even had a chance to say goodbye, to have any closure from losing her. To apologize because Riya had died because of her.

The sound of Jae rifling through some things brought her back to the present.

"Looks like they got my Linq," she said.

"They're probably working on breaking into it to find out where you might have run off to."

"Maybe. But Darshana wasn't specific when she messaged me. She used words only I could interpret when she told me to meet her."

He nodded. "Smart. I may be able to clone it, get your information and apps for you. Then I can deactivate the one they have, make it a brick. But I need my laptop to do that."

"Sounds good. Thanks." Mayhara headed for her bedroom to find the box that held her wristband. As she entered the small room, she took a look around, and part of her mind was saying goodbye to her things as she touched them, feeling grateful for having had them and apologizing for not being able to take care of them anymore. It was a maddening thing to have so much one moment only to lose it the next, but what she was most dismayed about losing was her freedom.

But maybe Jae was right; she had never really been free after all.

She opened her dresser and moved her clothes out of the way to find the box. She pulled it out, running her hand over the smooth surface before opening it. When she took out the garnet wristband and slipped it on, it was as if she'd found a part of herself that had been missing.

After she'd replaced the empty box in the drawer, she quickly threw together a bag of clothes. As she rejoined Jae in the living room, something caught her eye from under her couch among papers and books that the police must have tossed on the floor. She bent down and picked it up, remembering seeing it after she found Riya's body.

It was the strange, cryptic plastic card. She flipped it over in her hand, searching for something she might have missed.

"What's that?" Jae asked.

"I found it next to Riya's body. I don't know if it was hers." She shifted uncomfortably. "Or if it belonged to the masked man who attacked me."

"Mind if I take a look? If it belonged to your attacker, and he's part of the Pishacha, then we might have a lead."

She handed him the card, which he studied intently.

"There's a chip on the back. I think my Linq can read it."

She stepped closer to him, peering around his arm as his device scanned the chip.

"All I get is an address," he said.

They exchanged a look.

"Should we check it out?" she asked.

"It's the only lead we've got."

❦

When Jae brought the motorcycle to a stop, Mayhara stared at the building with its neon sign. A line of about fifty people dressed in tight, revealing clothes, waiting to be let in was snaked around the corner, and loud, thumping music vibrated through the air.

"A club?" Mayhara asked, still holding on to Jae's waist. "Are you sure this is the right address?"

"Yeah." Jae adjusted his grip on his handles. "You sure that wasn't Riya's card?"

"No way. This is so not her scene."

Jae shrugged. "Okay, let's find a place to park and check it out."

Jae leaned forward and drove the bike around the building to a full parking lot in the back. If he'd had a car, there would be no way he could have fit. He found space on a path near the back door, seemingly not concerned if he was allowed to park there or not.

Mayhara dismounted the bike and studied her clothes. "Well, this isn't going to do."

She grabbed her duffle bag that was strapped to the back of the motorcycle and rifled through it. Stripping off her hoodie to reveal a black tank top, she wrapped a choker around her neck—careful as she placed it over the bandage—and quickly tied her hair up in a messy bun. She then held up her hand. Small particles of crimson energy floated from her palm. The red dust settled, and Mayhara scooped it up with her finger. She then checked her reflection in Jae's motorcycle's mirror and smeared the red powder onto her lips, making a smacking sound with her mouth when she was finished.

"Better?" she asked.

Jae's mouth was agape as he looked her up and down. "That was so simple, yet so amazing."

She couldn't hold back her smile. "I'm just lucky I have my black jeans on. I hope they don't look as far as my shoes, though. They don't exactly scream 'club scene.'"

Jae gave her a crooked smile. "I'm sure you can figure out how to distract them from looking at your shoes."

She almost rolled her eyes at him, but he whipped out his Linq.

"It's Darshana," he said, his brow creased.

"Finally." Mayhara sidled up to him, trying to catch a glimpse of his screen. "What—none of that makes sense."

"It's code. Not that I haven't taken precautions, but she's being extra safe. She's lying low for a bit but tracking down the other mages."

Mayhara nodded. She wondered how many of the original elite mages were left. Knowing the crimson mage at the top of her class had been murdered caused her to believe the other mages were either in danger or already dead. She swallowed hard and stretched out her shoulders. She was going to have to be prepared for an attack. She couldn't let her guard down.

Jae shut down his screen.

"Wait," Mayhara said, placing her hand on his arm. "I need to know what your sister looks like. What if she's in there? I need to know who to look for."

"Good idea." He unlocked his Linq and opened a photo album, swiping until he found the picture he was looking for. "Here's one. This is from last year. Before Kashmeru found her."

He frowned as he added the last part. It took a lot for Mayhara to tear her gaze away from his sad eyes and examine the picture on his Linq instead.

In the picture, Jae had his arm around a beautiful, petite girl with bone-straight, light brown hair that cascaded down past her shoulders. They were both smiling, and they both had the same twinkle in their eyes. It looked like they had just shared a joke and captured the moment. Jae appeared relaxed and at peace. Naree looked like she was invincible.

"It's a good picture," Mayhara said softly, peering up at Jae.

His smile was small as he thanked her and tucked the Linq away. He gestured over his shoulder toward the club. "Let's see what we can find in there."

Fifteen

Mayhara's heart sank as they got to the end of the line. They could barely see the entrance from where they were standing, and at the slow pace the line was moving—if it was even moving at all—it was going to take forever to reach the door.

From the look on Jae's face, he was equally impatient. *Of course he is*, she thought to herself. *He desperately wants to find his sister.*

Suddenly, Jae stiffened. He moved closer to Mayhara, ducking his head down a little and shifting to face her. He lifted his arm as if scratching the hair at the top of his head. Looking past his bicep, Mayhara spotted the imperial police car that drove by the block. There were no sirens or flashing lights. Instinctively, Mayhara reached for her neck, running her fingers along the bandage. She had to remind herself that the blocking chip had been removed. It was halfway to New China by now.

As the patrol car continued on its way, Mayhara released a relieved breath. Jae checked over his shoulder to see the coast was clear, then let his arm fall as he stretched out his neck.

"All right," he said. "This is ridiculous. Maybe I could speed things along." He pulled out his Linq.

"How? What are you going to do?"

His eyes darted between her and his Linq for a moment, and then he swung an arm around her, pulling her closer.

When she shot him a questioning look, he leaned close to her ear. "Just trust me."

He held the Linq out at arm's length. The way they were standing, it appeared as if like they were simply taking a selfie. But the screen on his Linq showed one of the bouncers by the door. He was monitoring the line, his huge arms crossed over his muscular chest. In a matter of seconds, Jae zoomed in on the bouncer's face. His Linq captured his image.

Jae drew his Linq back and began pressing and swiping at it. Mayhara tried to see exactly what he was doing, but the angle was off. She only managed to catch a glimpse of a green square blinking over the bouncer's face and a file popping up.

Jae studied the words on his screen quickly, and then the corner of his mouth crept upward.

"Okay," he said, tucking his Linq away. "I've got it."

Jae took Mayhara's hand and stepped out of line.

"What are you doing?" she asked.

He pulled her along gently but quickly toward the door, and she had to move her feet to keep up. She made herself ignore the suspicious looks they were getting from the people they were passing in line.

When they got closer to the bouncer, Mayhara felt flustered. She wished Jae would have let her in on his plan.

The bouncer narrowed his eyes at them. He uncrossed his arms and stood akimbo.

"Line ends back there," the bouncer said.

"Freddy," Jae called out. "It's me, Rick."

The bouncer blinked, his eyes drifting over Jae's face as if trying to remember who he was. "Rick? I don't think—"

Jae leaned closer to him and lowered his voice. "You know, from the factory."

Freddy blanched for a moment, visibly swallowed, then checked over his shoulder to see if his colleague was listening. When he turned back to Jae, his expression had a hint of worry. "Keep it down, man."

"Yeah, yeah," Jae said, almost speaking out of one side of his mouth. "I got you, don't worry. Man, you think you can let us through? You know, as a favor? I had your back back at the factory, man. We all did."

Freddy looked back and forth between Jae and his colleague, the gears in his head clearly whirling. "Yeah, okay. You got it, man. But keep it down about back then, all right?"

"Of course, of course."

Freddy held his arm out to clear a way for Jae and Mayhara, then stepped forward and blocked the next people in line.

"VIP," he said to his colleague.

His colleague scanned their faces but didn't argue.

Jae held tight to Mayhara's hand as they squeezed past the people in line and into the entrance of the club. The music grew louder and the flashing neon lights pulsated faster. Streams of cold, white smoke blew turrets of clouds onto the floor as they passed the coat check and continued into the main chamber of the club.

It was hard to hear anything but thumping, and Jae had to repeat what he said before Mayhara could understand him.

"I *said*, 'Let's check by the bar,'" he said into her ear.

She simply nodded, not wanting to raise her voice.

A couple of young women dressed in what looked like streams of bandages wiggled in front of them, whooping and cheering and handing them tiny plastic cups of green liquid. Mayhara smiled and waved them away. Jae directed his focus over their heads, his eyes on the bar. He scanned the faces of the patrons, his frown deepening as he seemed to realize his sister was nowhere in sight.

"Let's ask the bartender," he said.

They shimmied to the bar and managed to squeeze between people.

"What can I get you?" the bartender asked.

Jae held out his Linq with the picture of Naree showing. "You seen this girl?"

The bartender raised a brow at him. "Maybe."

Jae pursed his lips and shook his head. "How much?"

The bartender opened a bottle of beer and handed it to the man next to Jae. Then he leaned closer. "Fifty."

Jae pressed a few buttons on his screen and held it out toward the bartender. The bartender touched the head of his Linq to the head of Jae's. The two devices let out beeps, and the men tucked their Linqs away.

"Yeah, I've seen her. She's in the VIP room." He pointed to a spiral stairway at the corner of the club.

"Any help getting up there?" Jae asked.

"Sorry, dude. It's gonna cost you more than fifty for that, and you'll have to speak to the boss, Bruno, to make that happen, and Bruno's off for the night. He's actually up there himself and asked not to be disturbed. Unless you've got an access card, but they are rare to come by. Good luck, though."

Jae nodded his thanks to the man and turned away from the bar.

"We're going up there?" Mayhara asked.

"We'll figure out a way."

She looked over his shoulder. Under the staircase, there was short hallway leading to a door. She could just make out the word ADMINISTRATION marked on the metal.

"I have an idea," she said. "That is, if you're as good a hacker as you seem."

"Tech prodigy."

She gave him a crooked smile. "There's a lock pad right outside the office door. Think you could break in?"

He followed her line of vision past the hoard of dancing bodies and narrowed his eyes. A smile slowly formed on his lips. "Yeah, I think I could." He glanced down at her. "We're going to have to do a little role-playing, though, so we don't get caught."

She held back a nervous laugh. "All right."

He placed a hand on the small of her back and steered her toward the office hall. Inching closer as they continued to walk, he bent his head until his mouth was right behind her ear. "Just warning you. We're going to have to get a little cozy."

The vibration of his voice on her skin caused goose bumps to erupt all over her body.

Get a grip, she told herself. *This is just for show.*

When they reached the hall, Mayhara looked up at Jae, not knowing what his plan might be.

Jae's eyes were on the lock pad. He pulled his Linq out of his pocket along with a short, black wire—the same one he'd used to crack the holding cell lock. "It'll take a moment to get the code, so we're going to have to make it look like we have a reason to be here. Even if that reason is—"

"To find a private place to make out?"

She bit back a laugh as his cheeks tinged with red.

"Yeah, uh…"

"Don't worry. I'm sure we can make it look convincing." Holding his arms, she positioned herself so her back was to the lock pad. There was just enough room for him to hook up his Linq. She took his head and directed it to her neck, giving him a view of the lock pad while making it appear to anyone who might come along that there was something else going on.

Playing her part, she ran her hands along his shoulders, every once in a while letting her fingers comb through the back of his hair. She kept her eyes on the end of the hall, making sure no one was coming, but a small part of her couldn't believe how amazing he smelled.

Behind her, the lock pad chirped, and the door clicked open.

Jae slowly lifted his head and slid his forehead against her temple. "Are we clear?"

She checked once more before meeting his eyes. "Yep."

He took her hand, glancing over his shoulder once before slipping in the door with her.

Mayhara tapped the control panel and pressed the button for the lights. The office was small, barely big enough for a desk, a bookcase, and a ratty-looking chair. Mayhara went over to the computer and found a metal box. Inside were plastic cards identical to the one she'd found in her apartment.

"The card I found," she said to Jae. "It's an access card."

Jae joined her, running his hand over a small machine standing next to metal box. "Okay, it's probably activated. Which means we need one more."

He hit a button on the keyboard, and the computer monitor came to life.

"You think you can get in?"

He scoffed. "Tech Prodigy 101."

She hovered over him as he sat in the chair and began typing away at the keyboard. She wasn't sure what he was doing, but windows were being opened on the screen and Jae started accessing files.

"Okay. Found it," he said. "Stick one of those cards in the reader."

She did what he'd asked, and as the machine made a buzzing sound, her eyes flitted over a few hanging pictures on the wall. One picture in particular caught her attention.

"Hey, check that out," she said.

Jae followed her gaze. "Is that the chief of police?"

"Yeah. With his arm around… Bruno, I'm guessing."

"No way." Jae seemed to go pale.

"You don't think that's him?"

"No, I do. It's just… that's him. That's the guy Naree's been seeing."

"Your sister's involved with Bruno? Wait, Darshana said the commander of the shadow army—"

"Bhutano," Jae said."

"Yes. Bhutano—that he's possessed a human body to lead the Lotus to Kashmeru's tomb. So Bruno is…

Bhutano?"

Jae rubbed at his chin, glaring at the picture. "It makes sense. He and the police chief appear pretty chummy. Makes me even more convinced the imperial police are connected to the Pishacha. Assuming Bruno is being possessed by Bhutano."

"He's got to be. Right?"

"There's got to be a reason they brought Naree here. It has to have something to do with the Pishacha." Jae shook his head as he took the activated card out of the machine. "But I can't connect the dots yet. What are they waiting for? Why not just bring Naree to Kashmeru's tomb and bring him back to life?"

"There must be more to the story." Mayhara squinted at the picture. "Wait."

"What?"

"The guy on the other side of Bruno. I swear he's the officer I saw at my office. He had a meeting with the director."

Jae shook his head. "I think this whole thing involves more people than we think."

"Is there anything on the computer that might give us a clue?"

"I'm copying the files to my cloud. We can check them out on my Linq later when we're not in a compromised situation."

"We need to get a hold of Darshana, too. See what she knows."

"Yeah." He stood, holding up the access card. "But first, let's try to rescue my sister."

They switched off the computer and headed out of the office, checking to make sure no one was paying any attention. They kept close together for show and went straight for the staircase.

Before they reached it, someone caught Mayhara's wrist. She pivoted quickly, her eyes widening upon seeing who it was who'd grabbed her.

"Rajev?"

"Mayha, I didn't expect to see you here." Rajev's smile didn't reach his eyes. "I've been trying to get ahold of you. You haven't answered any of my messages."

Jae stepped closer to Mayhara, his shoulders squared. Rajev's insincere smile disappeared completely.

"I don't have time to talk to you, Rajev," said Mayhara. "In fact, it's probably better if we cut ties altogether."

"What? Baby—" He reached for her.

"I'm not your baby," Mayhara said, slapping his hand away. "You stole from me."

"Borrowed," he insisted. "I was going to pay you back, I swear."

"Really?" Jae asked.

Mayhara could just make out the blue glow on Jae's palm as he set his hand on Rajev's shoulder.

Rajev blanched. He made a futile attempt to back away from Jae, but something made him hesitate. Mayhara thought it might have something to do with Jae's powers.

"What were you really planning on doing?" Jae asked.

Rajev's brow crinkled. "I'm going to keep the credits. I had no intention of paying her back."

The color drained from Rajev's face.

Truth, Mayhara remembered. It was one of the powers of a sapphire mage.

Mayhara exhaled heavily through her nose. Instead of screaming at Rajev—which would have been her kneejerk reaction—she contained herself, just like Darshana had taught her. If Jae could use his powers on Rajev, so could she.

"Raj," she said, placing her hand on his other shoulder and feeling invigorated as her palm glowed red, "I hope this bothers you for a long time. Forever, in fact, so you never do it to anyone else, ever again."

She squeezed his shoulder, and Rajev's knees gave out. He crumpled to the floor, still conscious, but struggling to get his bearings.

Stability. Or rather the ability to manipulate it. One of the crimson mage's powers.

"Let's go," Mayhara said to Jae. "He's wasted enough of our time."

Mayhara wasn't sure it would work, but she put on an expression of confidence as she led the way up the spiral staircase. It only crossed her mind for a split second that Jae might be watching her backside as they climbed.

At the top of the staircase, behind a small table, sat a young woman with bright pink hair in high-set pigtails. She chewed her gum with her mouth open, and from the expression on her face, Mayhara gathered there were other places she'd rather be.

"Are you on the list?" the girl asked.

"We've got these." Jae held out the cards.

The woman seemed bored as she took the cards and

slipped them, one at a time, into the reader machine on her table. The machine's green light lit for each card. "Yeah, okay."

She pressed a control panel at the table and the door to the VIP room opened. Mayhara gave Jae an apprehensive look before they stepped forward.

The room was long, with couches sectioning off small areas. It was only slightly less full than the chamber downstairs, but the music wasn't as loud. The lights in the VIP room ran on a slowly changing loop of light pink to deep purple to ocean blue and back again. Servers walked around with trays of drinks and small plastic cubes. Mayhara's guess was that the cubes held drugs in them, but she couldn't be sure.

A few of the patrons looked their way, but it wasn't until they reached the far end of the room that heads began to turn toward them with concern.

A young woman with long hair turned their way, following everyone's gaze. Mayhara gasped.

"That's her," she said.

"Naree!" Jae called out.

Naree stood, perplexed for a moment. Her eyes were like jewels. She stared at her brother. She was more beautiful in person than in the photo. She had an aura around her that was magical, and Mayhara couldn't help but be in awe of her presence.

Their view of her was quickly obscured by two tall men in black leather jackets and black mouth masks.

Jae set his jaw. "I'd like to speak with my sister."

One of the men pulled out a gun. "That's not going to happen."

Jae lifted his palms. Mayhara stiffened but readied herself.

The guys in the leather jackets drew their brows down and stepped forward. Behind them, one of the men beside Naree—Mayhara recognized him as Bruno from the picture in the office—grabbed her by the waist and led her quickly toward a rear door.

"Bruno?" Naree whispered.

"Let's go," he said, rushing her out the door.

The man with the gun aimed. Mayhara instinctively pushed out energy with her hands. Crimson particles shot out toward the gun just as the man moved to pull the trigger. The barrel was quickly jammed with red crystals, causing the gun to explode from the man's hand.

The second man lunged forward.

Jae grinded his teeth and raised his palm. Bright blue energy crystals began to form. Before he could generate enough sapphire particles to form an energy sphere, the two leather-jacket-clad men jumped him, one of them delivering a blow to his stomach.

Patrons around them were agitated and scared, some of them running for the main door of the VIP room to escape while others cowered beneath their tables.

Mayhara's blood grew hot with her mage powers. She shot off her crimson energy, hitting the nearest guy in the shoulder. He let out a yelp of pain as he was propelled backward, off of Jae. Without hesitating, Mayhara burst another crimson sphere at him, this one hitting him directly in the chest.

By this time, Jae had gained the upper hand on the other attacker, generating enough sapphire energy to hurl the man off of him and through the air. The man crashed into a table, his flailing legs knocking down a couple of chairs.

"Cover your ears," Jae said.

"What?" Mayhara asked, thrown by his request.

"Cover your ears!"

She did as he asked. As the two thugs struggled to get

up, Jae clapped his hands together, his palms glowing blue. The air around his hands vibrated visibly, like a circular disruption in the space around them, expanding outward. It was coupled with a harsh ear-popping thrum. The two men screamed in agony, slapping their hands over their ears as they crumpled to the ground.

Sound, Mayhara remembered. Part of the sapphire mage's powers.

"Come on." Jae grabbed Mayhara's hand and ran for the rear door, clearly not bothered with whether or not the two attackers would get up again. "They can't be far."

The rear door opened into a narrow hallway. At the end of the hall was an emergency exit door swinging closed.

Jae and Mayhara ran for the door, and Jae's hand caught it right before it slammed shut. They found themselves at the top of a fire escape. Bruno must have known that opening the door wouldn't set off the alarm. Mayhara hurried to the edge of the railing just in time to see Bruno holding Naree by her shoulders. She couldn't hear what he was telling her, but they both looked up when Jae called, "Naree, wait!"

A black jeep racing through the back lot skidded to a stop beside Naree and Bruno. Jae and Mayhara raced down the metal steps of the fire escape, but by the time they reached ground level, the jeep raced off and Naree was gone.

Bruno faced Jae and Mayhara, reaching behind his back and under his jacket. He pulled out a long, black, metallic, stick-like object. There was a click when Bruno's thumb shifted, and the stick extended into a pole. When Bruno swung it, it made a low, hollow hum.

Jae grit his teeth and opened his palms, ready to defend himself—or attack. Mayhara followed suit and brought her crimson energy to her palms.

Bruno advanced, holding the pole in front of him with both hands. Jae put one foot forward as he formed an energy sphere and quickly shot it toward Bruno. Bruno twirled the pole. The air hummed with its rotation. When the sphere got close to Bruno, the pole somehow stopped and dispersed the energy particles, making them spark and crackle in the air as they disappeared.

Mayhara's eyes widened. By the look on Jae's face, she wasn't the only one surprised by the function of this weapon.

Mayhara's garnet glowed on her wristband. Her power amped up, she hurled crimson energy at Bruno, hoping her sphere could penetrate the pole's shield. But as crimson particles broke apart and spread, crackling into the air around them, she knew it was of no use.

Bruno smirked, knowing he had the upper hand.

But it was two against one; surely, they could sway the odds in their favor.

Bruno lunged forward, this time with the pole's end aimed at Jae. Jae crouched and spun to the side, avoiding the pole's impact, but Bruno swung the pole to the side, its metallic end catching Jae in the arm. The sound of ripping fabric resonated in the air at the same time as Jae's outcry of pain. He staggered back.

Mayhara whirled a crimson sphere at Bruno, putting a spin on it in hopes it would get past his weapon.

Bruno swung the pole but only caught part of Mayhara's sphere. A good portion of crimson energy hit Bruno on the side of his head, throwing him off-balance.

With an angry shout, Bruno advanced on Mayhara. She sidestepped the pole, turning and catching it in her hands as she thrust Bruno into a nearby car. Her palm glowed red, but Bruno whipped the pole out of her hands and swiped it down and to the side, catching her legs. She emitted just enough crimson energy to knock him off his feet as she fell. A clattering sound reached her ears. She thought it was Bruno's pole, but he still held it in his hands.

Suddenly, Jae was on top of him. Jae's face was red with fury. He grabbed Bruno around the neck and slammed him into the ground.

"Tell me where my sister's gone!"

At first Bruno was shocked from the impact of his head against the ground, but then his eyes narrowed, and an eerie smile spread over his face.

Jae pulled his arm back, his fist glowing, ready to throw a punch. Before he could, thick black smoke filled the space where Bruno had been lying. Jae fell forward, holding on to nothing.

The smoke cleared. Bruno had disappeared.

Mayhara's breath left her. She felt as if all the blood had drained from her brain. He was gone. Just like that. In a huge cloud of black smoke.

"Shit!" Jae dragged his hands over his face, his skin going red.

"What?" Mayhara shook her head. "How?"

Jae let out a guttural scream, pulling at his hair. Mayhara placed her hands on her cheeks, forcing herself to keep calm, to think logically.

She stretched her neck, looking up at the night sky. The hazy streak of the Akutake comet caught her eye.

No. She couldn't let their destiny unfold in such a way. She had to make sure they stood a chance.

"Wait." Mayhara straightened and rushed to the nearby car. She bent down and reached under it, remembering the clattering noise she'd heard during the fight. When she got to her feet, a small smile surfaced on her face. She held up Bruno's Linq. "We're not lost yet."

Sixteen

aree's heart pounded in her throat. Her mind was clouded, and only one thought propelled her forward.

Kashmeru.

She couldn't resist him any longer. There was no reason for them to be apart. It was destiny.

The jeep sped down the highway, closer to their destination.

You know what you have to do.

She closed her eyes and nodded, having no choice but to do Kashmeru's bidding.

Bring me the dagger, and soon we will be together.

She opened her eyes, and suddenly a calm fell over her. She could do this. She would. For him. For her love. Nothing could keep them apart anymore. It was destiny. And she had no choice but to fulfill it.

Seventeen

Jae hissed through his teeth as Mayhara dabbed ointment onto the cut on his shoulder.

"Nearly done," she said softly, wrapping a bandage around the wound. She taped it off and packed up the first aid kit, stowing it on the shelf of Jae's small bathroom.

They'd gone to his apartment for recon after Bruno had disappeared. Jae wanted to read the files he'd copied from Bruno's computer as well as break into his Linq. Between the two sources, they hoped they could get a lead on where Naree might have been taken.

Jae stood, rotating his shoulder. With a wince, he pulled his shirt on. Mayhara found herself staring and quickly averted her gaze, turning to the sink to wash her hands.

"I forgot how invigorating it was," she said.

He tilted his head slightly, a look of bemusement on his face. "What?"

She wiped her hands off on the towel next to the sink, smiling at the sight of her wristband. "Using my powers without the pain."

The corner of his mouth inched upward. "Nothing quite like it."

"I mean, I probably shouldn't have used mage powers on Rajev." Darshana had always encouraged peace, emphasizing that mages should only use their powers in defense. "That was probably uncalled for."

Jae walked past her into the hall, continuing toward his living room. "You shouldn't feel bad about what you did to Rajev. If you ask me, he deserves a little destabilization."

She smirked. "I know. He's probably fine now, anyway. Even if it is with one thousand of my credits."

He stopped at the makeshift workstation his coffee table had become. "I can get them back for you."

"Yeah?"

"Of course. And if the authorities locked your accounts, I know a trick or two to unlock them and make it impossible to manipulate your records."

"You can do that?"

"No problem." He knelt in front of his laptop. "You need a little extra for the trouble?"

She laughed, resting her weight on the edge of his sofa. "Tempting, but no. Just what I earned fair and square."

"Mayhara, you work for the government. They don't deal with fair. You probably deserve ten times whatever they pay you. Minimum."

"Paid. Past tense. I'm pretty sure I've been fired at this point." She didn't want to think about her job. She bent her head, feeling disheartened. "I've been saving whatever I could for when I could get my family out of the prison camp. But I guess that's far from reality now."

Jae looked up at her with empathetic eyes, but he

didn't say anything. She knew he couldn't promise her anything. Neither of them could know how this would turn out.

Feeling the need for distraction, she glanced around the room, her eyes landing on a Celadon vase engraved with a lotus. Beside it sat a Korean *Hoon-ro* incense burner, and hanging on the wall, staring back at her, was a *Hahoetal*—a Korean folk mask made of alder wood and used in dances and plays, but which were also regarded as good-luck talismans.

The seemingly intense stare of the mask made her shift in her seat. "What do you think happened to Bruno?" she asked.

Jae didn't look up at her, busy concentrating on breaking into Bruno's Linq. "If I had to guess, I'd say it's some kind of magic connected to Bhutano's spirit."

"Kashmeru's main henchman. Right. But, disappearing *with* Bruno's body? I wouldn't think a spirit needed one. Or maybe it's like a parasite and can't survive without a host."

"I don't know how it works. Just like you, this is my first rodeo. And someone forgot to tell us how to break in our chaps."

She stood, stretching out her back. "Yet another mystery we hope Darshana can explain."

As she was about to head to the window to check the street, a ping emanated from Jae's laptop.

"What's that?" she asked.

"I've set an alert so I can be notified if the media reports anything about the prison camps."

He opened a new window on his screen and turned up the volume.

"*...centered around the possible uprising in the prison camps. One such extremist group came head to head with authorities at the Murwara prison today. While the imperial guards managed to get the attack under control, it wasn't without a few casualties. One guard and four prisoners lost their lives in the fight.*"

Jae looked up at Mayhara, concern etched in his features. "Is that where your family is?"

She slowly crossed her arms over her chest. "No. But it's only a matter of time. That's the third prison camp this has happened at. I don't know how these extremists are spreading through the system, but it terrifies me that my family will one day get caught in the crossfires."

"Something tells me your family knows to avoid the extremists," he said confidently. "Unless these extremists start camp-wide riots, your family should remain safe."

Mayhara's eyes were drawn back to Jae's monitor, where a picture of her was suddenly displayed on the news channel. Though she knew it was inevitable, it was still a shock to see herself on the screen.

"…has escaped from New Jaipur prison. We encourage all citizens to be on the lookout for the fugitive. Guatama is reported to be armed and dangerous. Anyone with information on her whereabouts should contact the imperial police immediately."

She looked down at her hands. Well, it wasn't exactly a lie. Her hands could be considered weapons. It didn't matter that she'd been taught to only use them to defend herself or to keep the Lotus empress safe. The authorities wouldn't care about that fact; she was a fugitive, and they would take her down at all costs.

Jae looked up at her. "I'm going to go ahead and say you're definitely fired."

She traced her garnet stone with a finger. "Now everyone will be keeping an eye out for me."

Jae rubbed the space under his bottom lip, studying her. "I've got a hat you can wear."

Despite the gravity of the situation, she let out a laugh. "You're a mastermind of disguises. Who knew?"

He stood, and for a moment Mayhara had forgotten how tall he was. She took a step back.

"But seriously," he said. "I've got some clothes here that belong to my sister. Some things she left the few times she crashed here—which was any time she needed to escape our overprotective parents."

He gestured for her to follow him as he made his way down the hall.

"I mean, I get it," she said. "That's a lot of pressure for her to have on her. And your parents. They were probably hard pressed to make sure no harm would come to her in any shape or form, and even if they were overprotective purely out of love, I imagine it can be suffocating."

Jae led her into the apartment's solitary bedroom— his bedroom—and opened up a drawer. He pulled out a pile of clothes and handed them to her. "Here are a few of her things. You can see what fits."

She stood there for a moment, staring at the clothes in her hands.

"What?" he asked.

"I don't know. It's just a little weird. Wearing the Lotus empress's clothes."

He smirked. "She's also just a girl, with normal thoughts and feelings, same as you. Don't let it get to you so much."

She nodded. "Yeah. Yeah, okay. Thanks."

He gave her a reassuring nod as he left the room. In the silence he left behind, Mayhara took in a deep breath and blew it out slowly. She smoothed her hand over the soft blouse on the top of the pile, trying to wrap her head around what her life had become.

When she had trained at the academy, she used to fantasize about what it would be like to serve the new Lotus empress. Having walked the corridors of the palace, it had been easy to imagine dressing in the imperial mage garb, her uniform of crimson and black always freshly ironed as the crimson mage cadets did their part to ensure peace in the palace and across the land. Of course, back then she'd always imagined being under the wing of Fei

Ling, the elite crimson mage during her training years. Now Fei Ling was gone, the Lotus empress in the hands of the Pishacha, and Mayhara was on the run, wearing the Empress's clothes.

After she was dressed, she folded her clothes away neatly and set them on the corner of Jae's bamboo dresser. His bed—which sat low to the floor—was neat, but not made to perfection. She imagined his priorities lay more with finding his sister rather than making sure his place was pristine. For a split second, she had the urge to run her hands over his duvet to straighten it out. Instead, she cleared her thoughts and left his room.

She found him hunched over the equipment on the coffee table. A mug of steaming liquid sat next to his laptop. A short black cable ran from the laptop to Bruno's Linq. A program was opened showing a sequence of running numbers and letters. Mayhara guessed this was the software Jae used to hack into password-protected equipment.

"Any luck?" Mayhara asked.

"Getting closer," Jae answered. "I made us some tea." He gestured to the side table, where she spotted another mug.

"Thanks."

"Oh, and there's this." He handed her a Linq. "I got as far as the screen to connect it to your cloud. Go ahead and log in. It's untraceable, so you can download it onto there."

"You couldn't just hack into my cloud?" she teased.

"I only hack when I need to. I still respect your privacy."

She smiled at him. "Thank you. Believe me, I'm in a place where I could use a little feeling respected."

Next to her tea was a tiny plate with two *Ariselu*. She smiled, as she was fond of the sweet rice cakes. "Is this from the shop downstairs?"

"Yeah," he said, the hint of a smile touching his lips. "The kind old lady who owns the place took a liking to me. She rents me this place, which—as far as hidden apartments go— is a dream. And I help her out when she gets shipments in or needs help taking inventory."

"That's a nice setup."

"And her *Ariselu* are incredible."

Curiosity tugged at her. She took one of the cakes and indulged in a bite. "Oh, wow. Yeah, that's amazing."

She let him continue his work, enjoying the small

moment of hot tea and sweet rice. She knew it wouldn't last long and was determined to take it all in while she could.

"I think I found something in the files I copied from Bruno's computer," Jae said. "It's a folder with names and addresses. But it's a long list. It'll take forever to go through. And there's another file here with some locations and maps."

"You think they have something to do with the Pishacha?"

"I wouldn't rule it out."

The ping from his laptop made Jae sit upright. "I'm in."

Mayhara set down her tea and moved to kneel beside him, her eyes darting around at all the names on the files he had open on the laptop. "Looks like the Census Information we keep track of at work. These locations are all over New United Asia. What's the connection? Who are these people?"

Jae's attention was on Bruno's phone. "I got into his messages. There's a name on a recent one. Jungkong Pi. Looks like they were trying to find this guy."

She inched forward toward the monitor. "There."

She pointed at the name in the file. "Here's an address. Think we should check it out?" She waited as Jae typed the address into his Linq.

"Yeah," he said, getting to his feet. He held out a hand to help her up. "Let's go."

Jae grabbed a cloth beanie and a silk head scarf by the front door, handing the scarf to Mayhara. "You're probably going to want to hide your hair."

She nodded and wrapped the head scarf around her head, tucking the ends of her hair underneath it.

They left the apartment and descended the stairs that led to the *ariselu* shop. Jae placed his palms together and bowed to the shop owner, and he and Mayhara took the back door out to an alleyway. It was the same way through which they'd come, hidden and discreet. It explained how Jae was able to remain off the radar after he'd returned to New India from Korea.

Once they were out of the alleyway, they headed down the street, toward the rented garage where Jae kept his motorcycle. But halfway there, Jae came to a sudden stop.

"What?" Mayhara asked "What is it?"

Jae pointed ahead of them. "Aren't those the guys

from the club?"

Mayhara drew in a breath, recognizing the two men she and Jae had fought in the VIP room. They looked as if they were checking the shops and scrutinizing the passersby.

"Think they're looking for us?" Mayhara asked.

"Probably. Come on. We're going to have to get creative to get past them."

Jae led her across the street, the two of them keeping their heads down. Just as they slipped into a ramen noodle bar, causing the hanging bell on the door to ring, Mayhara glanced in the direction of the two men.

One of the men turned their way. His eyes widened and he yelled to his colleague.

Jae let out a curse as he put his hand on Mayhara's back and hurried her through the restaurant. The space between tables was tight, and in their rush, Mayhara's foot caught on the leg of one of the tables. She fell, and Jae nearly toppled over her. Waiters and cooks shouted at them, waving their arms around in anger, and then the bell above the door rang again as Bruno's men barged into the place.

Jae grabbed Mayhara's hand and tugged her to her

feet. Mayhara's knee slammed into a chair, but she had no time to complain. They dashed for the back door, squeezing through it and slamming it shut.

Mayhara held a palm against the door and concentrated. Crimson particles rapidly generated from her hand, the energy spreading along the seam of the door and hardening. Once the door was sealed, she stepped back, hoping it would hold. She barely heard the pounding and shouts from the other side of the door over the hammering of her heart. But her crimson seal held.

"Let's go," Jae said, taking her hand and leading her down the back alley.

Mayhara fought off the pain in her knee, focusing instead on their trek to the garage. She just hoped they could reach Jae's motorcycle before Bruno's buddies could find them.

Eighteen

Music played softly in the elevator as Naree made her way to the floor she'd been instructed to go to. She knew the apartment number. She knew what the man looked like.

There was only one more thing to do.

The elevator dinged as the doors opened, and Naree walked down the hall with confidence.

Soon she would be with her love. Soon she would feel his arms around her again, the soft feel of his lips on hers.

Soon, her destiny would be fulfilled.

She stopped in front of the door of her target and pressed the buzzer.

Only moments later, the man from the picture opened the door, gaping at her.

She wondered if he recognized her, but she couldn't be sure. There was no reason anyone would know who she was. She'd been hidden for so long. But perhaps those who secretly continued to work for the empire had spread the word about her existence.

"Can I help you?" the man asked.

"Yes," she said, stepping forward. "I believe you can."

Nineteen

The address in Bruno's Linq led them to a high-rise apartment building in Kuchaman City. It had been a grueling two-hour ride. When Mayhara wasn't checking over her shoulder to make sure they weren't being followed, she was gritting her teeth against the roughness of the highway. The previous war had left it in ruins, and the administration had done close to nothing to renovate. Even when she and Jae dismounted the motorcycle, Mayhara couldn't shake the feel of the vibrating bike. It was as if the buzzing was alive in her bones.

The only respite Mayhara felt was that perhaps, with the distance between their current location and New Jaipur, the news of her escape hadn't traveled this far.

After removing his helmet, Jae slipped on a baseball cap and signaled to Mayhara to put her head scarf on. She obliged, tucking her hair into it, and then pulled up the collar of her jacket for added discretion.

The high-rise was a compendium of activity, brought about mostly from the shops and café on the ground floor. There were so many people coming in and going out of the main entry that Mayhara was sure they could blend in.

When Jae headed for the stairwell, Mayhara didn't question him. It was too easy to be caught in an elevator. A stairwell gave them more escape routes, though she wasn't too thrilled about the fourteen-story climb. At least it wasn't twenty—or more.

When they reached Jungkong Pi's floor, Jae tugged the bill of his cap down, his eyes drifting momentarily to the security camera mounted in the corner of the hall. They were counting on the high-rise running on the same automated security system as most buildings. It would be to their advantage if no one was constantly monitoring the halls. Still, they hadn't done anything yet to strike suspicion.

Mayhara pointed to the number plate outside the apartment they were looking for. "Fourteen twenty-two," she whispered. "You think she's here?"

Jae clenched his jaw. "I don't know, but if not, maybe this Jungkong guy can give us some information about where she went. And what she's up to."

Jae seemed to be holding his breath as he knocked on the door.

Mayhara kept her ears pricked, waiting for some sign that someone was home. All she could hear was Jae quietly letting out a curse before he knocked again.

"No one's home," Mayhara said after another minute of silence.

Jae glanced discretely at the security camera before pulling out his Linq. He was quick about hooking up his wire to it and attaching the other end of the cable to the lock pad on Jungkong Pi's door. In a matter of seconds, the lock pad's light turned green, and the door clicked open.

Jae went in first, and Mayhara instinctively checked over her shoulder before following him in. They looked around the living room, unable to find anything unusual. Mayhara turned toward the kitchen, and Jae signaled that he would check the bedroom.

Finding a pile of papers on the kitchen counter, Mayhara decided to rifle through them to see if she could find anything that might help them, but she barely touched the pile before Jae called her from the bedroom.

She didn't like the sound of his voice, and dread tore through her as she rushed to find him. It was as if she knew what to expect when she stepped into the bedroom. On the floor, on the opposite side of the bed, lay a bloody body.

Mayhara's knees almost gave out, but she caught herself on Jae's arm.

"Oh my God," she said. "Is that him?"

"I think so. Looks like he was stabbed."

Jae moved forward, and Mayhara swept her fingers under her head scarf, wiping sweat from her temples. Crouching on the floor, Jae inspected the area around the body.

"I don't see a weapon," he said. When he surveilled the room, something caught his attention, and he stood.

"What is it?" Mayhara asked.

"A laptop on the desk." Jae hurried over to it. "The camera is facing the room. There's a program on, recording everything. It's still running."

"Recording?" Mayhara made her way to his side. "Why?"

"I can't be sure. But let's see what happened here."

She leaned a bit closer as he tapped at the keys. In a matter of seconds, he brought up the video feed that had been recording. A man—the same man that lay on the floor, except very much alive—sat facing the screen.

"Hello, this is Jungkong Pi, one of the Sacred Keys. I'm attempting to send this message to the other Keys. If you find this before hearing from me, it means I've fled… or I'm dead. The Pishacha are coming. We must protect the daggers from the Council of the Seven. Kashmeru has the Lotus, and he—"

On the video, a door buzzer could be heard. Jungkong Pi disappeared from the camera, but before he'd left his room, he had switched the direction of the camera to face his room, leaving the video recording. A woman's voice could be heard faintly in the background.

"Naree?" Jae whispered, recognizing the voice.

"*You are mistaken,*" Jungkong said off-camera. "*There's nothing here.*"

"*You're lying. Or did you forget I have all mage powers?*" Naree suddenly appeared on the video but didn't seem to notice she was being filmed. She began opening drawers in Jungkong's room, searching for something.

"*Empress, please,*" Jungkong said. "*I'm trying to protect you. To protect the universe.*"

She ignored him, bending down and pushing the rug aside. Jungkong's eyes widened. Naree dug her fingers into the grooves in the wooden floor and loosened a floorboard. Jungkong pounced, attempting to stop her. Naree raised her hand. Crimson particles shot out at him, knocking him back against the frame of his bed.

She then reached between the floorboards and pulled out a black box decorated in a shiny red-and-gold pattern. Jungkong got to his feet just as Naree opened the box and slipped out a large silver dagger.

This time when Jungkong jumped toward her, trying to grab the dagger, Naree turned it in his direction and thrust it toward him. Jungkong fell on it, his eyes widening and his mouth falling open. Blood surged from where he was stabbed, and he stumbled backward. Naree pulled the dagger out of him and stared at the blade. For a moment, she looked scared. Her breaths came out in gasps and her hands shook.

Then a strange glow appeared in her eyes. It went away almost as fast as it had come. Her expression went stoic, and she wiped the dagger on the rug, ridding it of Jungkong's blood.

She stood, as if in a trance, and left the room with the dagger in hand.

The rest of the footage showed nothing. Jae forwarded through the recording until it got to the part where he and Mayhara entered the room.

He clicked it off, then took a step back from the computer, his hand cupping his mouth and chin as his brow furrowed.

"That's… That's…" Mayhara couldn't even finish her sentence. She was so in shock from what she'd just seen. From the look on Jae's face, he was as well.

"We need to erase this," he said, his fingers flying to the keyboard. "If the authorities get ahold of this, Naree will be locked away forever."

Mayhara stayed silent as Jae erased the footage, her emotions in battle over whether it was right or wrong to tamper with evidence. There would clearly be a police investigation into Jungkong's murder, and Jae was deleting the proof the police would need. But she understood why he was doing it. Not only because Naree was his sister, but because Jae knew she wasn't in complete control of her actions. She was being used as a pawn for Kashmeru's gain.

A buzzing from Jae's pocket sounded. When Jae pulled out the Linq, Mayhara realized it was Bruno's. She read the message displayed on the screen, which came from someone named Ghazaar.

Bruno, where are you? First dagger acquired. Headed to the meeting point in Sariska. Better hurry. Bhutano is pissed. See you at Phong's.

Mayhara and Jae exchanged confused glances.

"Bhutano is pissed?" Jae shook his head. "But I thought Bruno was possessed by Bhutano. That means—"

"Bhutano is possessing someone else" Mayhara pressed her hands to her cheeks as she put the pieces together. "Bruno was just one of the Pishacha, probably assigned to protect Naree."

"And Bhutano is still out there."

They were quiet for a moment, pondering what this meant. Then Mayhara put a hand on Jae's arm.

"They don't know what happened to Bruno," Mayhara said. "Or that you have his Linq."

"On a positive note, it means Bruno hasn't resurfaced anywhere yet. If he does at all." Jae stood. "Guess we're going to Sariska." He took a handkerchief out of his jacket pocket and wiped down the keyboard.

Mayhara nodded, mentally preparing herself for the four-hour journey. As they left the apartment, her mind raced to make sure neither of them had touched anything else. She was already a fugitive, but if the police found her fingerprints at the scene of a crime, it could make her a target for a 'shoot-on-sight' situation.

They hurried down the stairwell, neither of them saying much. When they reached the lobby, it was even more busy than it had been when they'd arrived. Jae put his hand on Mayhara's back to make sure they stuck together as they squirmed their way through the throng of people.

Bright sunshine warmed Mayhara's face as they got outside the building. To everyone around them, it was a lovely day, business as usual. But Mayhara couldn't help but think there was a dead man in an apartment upstairs who would never feel sunshine again.

They rounded the corner, headed for where Jae had parked his bike. Mayhara collided into Jae's arm as he came to a sudden stop. Looking past him, she saw the police officer inspecting Jae's motorcycle. The officer had his tablet out, no doubt typing in the license plate number.

As the officer spoke into his radio, Jae turned to Mayhara.

"We're going to need to take the sub-train." He kept his voice down and peered over his shoulder as he directed Mayhara away from the street.

"The sub-train might get us there quicker anyway," Mayhara said. "But your bike—"

"Don't worry. I'll get it back later."

Jae checked his Linq and found the nearest sub-train station, which luckily was not too far away.

The day began to heat up, and Mayhara longed to remove the head scarf from her head but kept it on to be safe. She found herself ducking her head down and eying the ground any time they crossed paths with anyone in any kind of uniform. She was thankful that Jae was so confident and determined; it helped her stay focused on their mission, whereas otherwise, she would fall apart from being overwhelmed.

The sub-train station was packed, and they were lucky to get a standing place on the train, smooshed up against a dozen other passengers. When Jae looked down at his arm, Mayhara realized she'd been clinging to it. Instead of letting go, she looked up at him and offered him a small smile. The corner of his mouth turned upward, and Mayhara relaxed a little. She leaned a little closer, both because she was terrified of being recognized, but also because him being near comforted her.

After a couple of stops, Jae pulled Bruno's Linq out of his pocket. He worried his lip as he read the screen.

"What is it?" Mayhara asked quietly.

"Ghazaar. Looks like he's getting nervous about Bruno not answering him."

Mayhara smirked. "Well, maybe 'Bruno' should answer him then."

Jae gave her a sideways look, matching her smirk. "All right. 'Bruno' will let him know he's on the way."

He typed in the message quickly and tucked the Linq away. When his eyes met Mayhara's, they both let out a small laugh.

About an hour outside Kuchaman City, the sub-train had emptied enough for Jae and Mayhara to sit. Though part of her had gotten comfortable to be holding on to Jae for physical and emotional support, she was glad to finally be able to get off her feet.

The rocking movement of the sub-train lulled her into a tranquil, almost-numb state, and before she knew it, she was waking up, having fallen asleep on Jae's shoulder. She looked around, confused and self-conscious, trying to focus on how long she'd been asleep.

"Where are we?" she whispered to Jae. "I must have passed out."

"We're about an hour outside of Sariska. And don't worry about it. You needed the rest."

She adjusted her head scarf. "Have you been awake the whole time?"

"Yeah. I'm not tired. Just anxious."

She felt the urge to reach out and squeeze his hand, but she resisted. Instead, she took a look around, noting the passengers who were busy checking their Linqs or reading books. Her eyes came across a man at the far end of the train. He was dressed in black and a black mouth mask hung at his chin. Though she knew the Pishacha wore the masks, it wasn't uncommon apparel in New United Asia, so she couldn't be sure he was one of the shadow army or simply an innocent citizen. He looked away when their gazes met, but she could have sworn he was watching her. She pulled the scarf a little lower over her brow and crossed her arms over her chest, hugging herself.

Probably just my paranoia, she thought.

She looked toward the window, but they were still underground. Nothing to see but blackness. When she turned her head, her eyes met the mysterious man's again. Her muscles tensed, and she grabbed Jae's wrist.

"What?" he asked, his voice low.

She leaned closer to him and whispered, "I think that man is watching us."

She gestured with her eyes without turning her head.

Jae made sure not to look too quickly. Instead, he kept his eyes on her and reached for her cheek. Mayhara's breath caught, not knowing what he was about to do. He leaned in closer to her, his mouth nearing her ear, and when his breath touched her skin, a thrilling shiver traveled up her spine. With his face close to hers, he turned his head slightly, as if he were about to whisper in her ear, but his eyes went to where the mysterious man sat.

She let out a breath, understanding Jae's strategy, but still she couldn't shake the fact that she'd enjoyed his touch.

"Yeah," Jae whispered. "He's watching us."

"What should we do?"

"It might be nothing. Or he might recognize you from your picture on the news."

"Or he could be Pishacha." She swallowed back her nervousness. "Should we get off the train?"

She took a chance and glanced at the man. He squared his jaw and stood, sending Mayhara's heart into a panic. The man walked toward them, purpose in his gait, and reached into the pocket of his jacket. Mayhara instinctively opened her hands, ready to defend herself. Jae did the same. They stood.

With a quick movement, the man pulled something shiny out of his pocket and threw it down the aisle. He then pulled up the mouth mask, covering his nose and mouth as he continued toward Mayhara. As white smoke filled the sub-train, the passengers began to panic, getting up from their seats and heading for the opposite side of the train. But the passengers closest to the smoke were too late, their eyes rolling to the backs of their heads as they collapsed.

"It's some kind of chemical," Jae said, the white smoke pluming toward them.

Mayhara held out her palms and shot out a cloud of crimson energy as she and Jae backed away from the man. Her crimson cloud pushed the white smoke away from them, and Jae fired off sapphire shots at the man. One hit him in the chest, knocking him back. Mayhara continued to beat back the smoke with her particles.

Jae took her arm. "Come on."

He pulled her toward a nearby door and pulled the emergency handle. The sub-train shuddered and skidded to a stop, the cabins filling with a blaring alarm. Jae pried the door open with his hands, just enough for Mayhara and him to squeeze through. He blasted one more shot of sapphire at the man, who'd gotten to his feet. This time the energy hit him in the head.

Mayhara climbed out of the train, dropping to the side of the tracks in the underground tunnels. Jae dropped down beside her and pointed in the direction they needed to run. Mayhara didn't dare turn back, for fear it would slow her down.

They dashed through the darkness of the sub-train tunnels, headed for the next station. They darted past puddles and rats as they got farther away from the compromised sub-train. Jae pulled Mayhara back to the center of the tunnel between the tracks as another sub-train charged toward them. He held on tightly to her as the wind kicked up dust and dirt and debris around them. Mayhara closed her eyes, leaning into Jae until the sub-train passed.

"All clear," he finally said, and they darted down the tunnel again.

There was a light up ahead, and Mayhara felt relief fill her chest as they neared the station. When they reached it, Jae gave her a boost, and they both climbed to the platform.

It was only then that Mayhara dared to look back. She didn't see anyone coming, but she wasn't about to underestimate the man's determination to chase them down.

"We've got to get out of here," she said.

"This way up," Jae said, putting a hand on her back and urging her toward the escalator.

They ran up it, finding themselves on a quiet street. It appeared as if it was someplace just outside of the nearby city. There were only a few people around: a woman pushing a baby carriage on the sidewalk across the street, and a group of school kids in uniforms bantering and laughing as they headed home. Mayhara spotted the faint smudge of the comet above the town, reminding her of their urgency.

"Maybe there's a bus stop or something nearby?" she asked. "Or a taxi?"

"I don't want to risk a taxi driver recognizing you." Jae checked his Linq. "We're not that far from Sariska. There's a bus station about ten kilometers from here. We're going to have to walk."

Mayhara looked over her shoulder at the sub-train station entrance. "How about we walk quickly?"

Jae let out a small laugh. "All right. Sounds good."

Twenty

You've done well, my love.

Naree woke in the back of the jeep to Kashmeru's voice.

We're one step closer.

She'd done it for him. All her reincarnations had led to this one. This fated one where they would finally be united.

It was always the way.

She pressed her hands to her heart. She could almost feel him there. Her heart thrummed with the knowledge they would soon be together.

Her Kashmeru.

Her love.

There's one more thing I need to you do before we can continue, my love.

"Anything," she whispered. She could barely stand another second without him. "Just tell me what to do."

I knew I could count on you, my love.

Twenty-one

When they arrived in the Alwar district of Sariska, Mayhara wasn't sure what to expect. She had heard that the administration had plans to shut down the national park, but it didn't appear as if the town near the tourist attraction had been abandoned yet. The streets were still littered with patrons visiting the restaurants, cafés, and gift shops, as well as buying tickets to the tiger reserve.

Jae inspected the map feature on his Linq. "Phong's is a café a bit east of here." He pocketed his device and glanced at Mayhara. "Ready?"

"Yeah, let's go."

The town was surrounded by forests, grasslands, and rocky hills, with the road their bus had come in on snaking through the center of the tourist hotspots. Mayhara was actually grateful for the head scarf, which kept the hot sun off her scalp.

They approached the café, and Mayhara's mouth watered at the sight of the tall glasses of liquid set at the tourists' tables.

"Think we could get a drink?" she asked.

"Yeah, we probably should hydrate. Come on."

Mayhara first went to the restaurant's entrance, scoping out the tables inside. With no trace of Naree, they decided to grab a small table near the edge of the café's front terrace. They each ordered the 'delicious homemade lemonade' the café advertised, and when the drinks came, Mayhara couldn't indulge in hers quick enough.

With her thirst quenched, Mayhara felt more awake, more aware. She scanned the restaurant, wondering if they had missed Naree and Ghazaar. Perhaps they had tired of waiting for Bruno and left. But Jae hadn't gotten any more messages on Bruno's Linq, and he didn't want to initiate a message from 'Bruno,' just in case something he typed clued in Ghazaar that the messages were fake. They'd have to wait it out until they got another lead.

Jae called the waitress over and ordered two plates of *Masala Poha*, much to Mayhara's delight.

She raised a brow at him.

"We'll collapse if we don't eat anything," he said to her when the waitress walked away. "Might as well have some sustenance while we wait for them to show up."

The food came quickly, and Mayhara found herself devouring it. She had been so nervous about confronting the Pishacha, evading the police, and rescuing Naree, that she hadn't realized how hungry she was.

They polished off their meals while continuing to keep watch. Jae checked Bruno's Linq every few minutes, making sure it was actually on and the battery hadn't suddenly died.

After the waitress cleared their plates, Jae paid for the meal.

"I'm going to the ladies' room," Mayhara told him. "Be right back."

She almost felt dizzy leaving the table, but she figured it was her body catching up with everything she'd been through in the last couple of days. Her system was probably in a happy sort of shock from the food and drinks. A bit dazed in the ladies' room, Mayhara went through the motions while her mind wandered. When she stepped out of the bathroom stall, she grimaced at her reflection in the mirror. She desperately needed a shower. She pulled the head scarf down and almost laughed at her hair. She needed a brush. Or scissors.

She washed her hands and rubbed her wet fingers under her eyes and along her neck. Behind her, the door opened, and a woman walked in.

Not just any woman; it was Naree.

Naree must not have recognized her at first, because she continued to the sink beside Mayhara, rifling through her large purse in search of something.

And then it dawned on her. She froze, just as Mayhara was getting her wits about her to make a move. But in one split second, Naree threw out her palms. Her palms glowed green and before Mayhara could react, a sudden force of wind blew Mayhara back against the tile wall. Her head hit the hard surface, the ache making her squeeze her eyes shut for a second. When she opened them, Naree was gone.

Shouting a curse, Mayhara charged for the door. She looked around and caught sight of Naree hurrying through the kitchen entrance.

"Jae!" she shouted, not caring if the waiters or patrons were bothered by her outburst. She could barely make out his face out on the terrace. "She's getting away!"

Jae jumped up, and Mayhara turned on her heel. She dashed for the kitchen and spotted Naree escaping out the back door. The cooks and wait-staff yelled and hollered as she tore through the kitchen running after her. By the time Mayhara broke through the back door, Naree had slipped into the woods that bordered the restaurant's property.

Mayhara took off after her at top speed. She was barely aware that Jae was behind her, catching up. Her pulse hammered in her ears as she breached the line of trees. Jae was quickly beside her as they wound and weaved through the Kadaya, bamboo, and Dhok trees.

Naree looked over her shoulder, her brows drawn, and disappeared behind some large shrubs.

Suddenly, everything in Mayhara's vision went purple. She was blinded. She skidded to a stop.

"What's happening?" she asked, reaching out in hopes of finding Jae.

"She's using her powers to stop us."

Amethyst mage powers, Mayhara realized. Sight was one of them. And back in the ladies' room, Naree had used the emerald mage power of air to knock her back.

"It won't last," Jae said. "Trouble is, the magic diminishes the farther away she gets."

He cursed, obviously feeling defeated.

Mayhara reached out farther and found him. She took his hand. "We can catch up. Can you hear her?"

Instead of answering, he squeezed her hand. Through the purple haze, tendrils of blue energy snaked from what Mayhara could only assume was Jae's free hand.

"Okay," he said. "Watch your step."

Jae tugged on her hand, and she had no choice but to move one foot in front of the other to keep up with him. She kept a hand out to be sure she wouldn't collide with a tree, but she wasn't too sure her foot wouldn't catch on a twig or slip into a hole in the ground.

After a minute of seeing nothing but purple, the air started to clear. It was as if Jae had magically appeared out of nowhere, even though he had been guiding her the entire time. She trusted he was still listening for his sister since he seemed to be confident of which direction to go.

Up ahead, between breaks of the camouflage of trees, glowing eyes locked with hers. Something shiny gleamed from Naree's hand.

The dagger, Mayhara thought.

Naree quickly turned away from them as she slipped into a darker part of the forest. As they neared the spot where she'd disappeared, Mayhara realized it was the entrance to a cave situated in a rocky hill.

"Naree!" Jae called out, stepping forward through rocks and shrubs.

Mayhara surveilled the entrance. It appeared as though the rocky ground descended to lower depths under the hill. Even using her crimson mage powers of feeling the earth, there was no telling how deep this cave went. And there was no telling what awaited them inside.

But there was no question as to whether or not they would go after Naree. She was Jae's sister and the Lotus empress. They had no choice.

Inside, there were a few spots of light, where the sun shone through breaks in the rock above them. There were tunnels ahead, and a howling wind pushed through every now and then.

Jae listened and pointed to the tunnel on the right. "This way."

Instinctively, Mayhara opened her hands. Her palms glowed red. Jae placed a hand on her arm.

"Wait. We don't want to hurt her." He swallowed hard. "She's my sister. She might not be in the right mind to remember that, but it's still Naree inside."

"Of course," Mayhara said. "I don't want to hurt her, either."

He nodded and they moved toward the tunnel.

Mayhara tried to keep her breathing quiet so Jae could listen for his sister. As she looked around, the rocky walls reminded her of a tomb.

"Do you think this is where Kashmeru's body is buried? It would explain why they came to Sariska and why Naree brought the dagger here."

"I don't know. It's possible. I know there are a lot of temples around here. Seems fitting for the tomb of a deity. There's even a ghost town not far from here—as in occupied by actual ghosts."

Shivers crawled up Mayhara's arms. She hadn't really thought about it, but now that he'd said it, there was a chance they would be dealing with the spirit of Kashmeru. She wasn't sure if she was an elite enough mage to confront him.

The tunnel opened up, revealing a small cavern with an elevated level in front of them that led to another tunnel. In front of that tunnel stood Naree. In one hand, she held the dagger. Her other hand was raised and glowed red.

"No. Naree!" Jae put his hands up, but not to use his powers. "It's me—Jae! Don't—"

There was a blank stare in Naree's eyes, and Mayhara knew she wasn't in control. She wouldn't respond to her brother's words.

Crimson energy spilled out from Naree's palm, and the ground rumbled beneath them.

Mayhara and Jae struggled to keep their balance as the earth quaked. Mayhara fell to the side, scraping her arm as she hit the ground. Jae tripped to the opposite wall. The ground between them cracked and crumbled, the rumble growing louder.

On the upper level, Naree turned and ran into the tunnel.

Jae and Mayhara got to their feet on unsteady legs as

the earth continued to shake, and the crack between them grew until it became a huge gap. Mayhara looked over the edge, but all she saw was a bottomless hole that separated her from Jae. She put her hand up, ready to use her mage powers to create a crimson-particle bridge to get to him, but the second she called upon her magic, an eruption of golden fire burst from the crevice. She shielded her face from the heat of the flames.

She looked back the way from which they'd come, but the earth had fallen into the crevice there. She couldn't turn back. She could go forward, though. There was a place where she could form a bridge to the upper level so she could go after Naree. But it was impossible to get to Jae, at least with the fire dancing its great heights between them. She doubted her crimson particles could withstand the Lotus's golden fire magic. It appeared he was trapped.

"Jae!" Mayhara shouted. "Can you move anywhere? Back toward the entrance, maybe?"

For a second, he didn't answer, and Mayhara feared he might be hurt or unconscious.

"Yes," he finally said. "I can go back. I'll try to take the other tunnel near the entrance and see if I can catch up."

"I'm going after Naree," she said through the flames.

"Hopefully, one of us will be able to find her."

"Be careful!"

"You too!"

Mayhara stayed close to the stone wall, as far away from the flames as she could. She threw out her powers and formed a crimson bridge to take her to the upper level, and then raced forward to the tunnel Naree had run through.

She was plunged into darkness. She held her hands in front of her, using the glow of her palms as a source of light. It wasn't much, but at least she wasn't completely blind. She moved through the tunnel as quickly as she could, but it seemed to go on forever.

The terrain was uneven, and she had to stop now and then to catch her breath. Sweat covered her temples and back, and she wasn't sure her powers would hold out long enough for her to keep the glow of her palms going. Depleted and exhausted, she gasped when she spotted light up ahead.

Her pace picked up, and a sense of hope overcame her as she reached the end of the tunnel. It opened up into a chamber. The floor of the chamber shimmered, and there was a break in the ceiling of the cave, casting a pool of light onto the center, which refracted the light into the large space. It was as if millions of sparkles danced in the air.

She moved forward slowly, glancing around in search of Naree, squinting from the brightness of the sparkles. Footsteps to her left made her turn, and she instinctively held her palms up but didn't call upon her powers. Her tense shoulders dropped in relief when she spotted Jae running toward her.

"You made it," she said, resisting the urge to throw her arms around him.

"It was a challenge," he said as he panted. "Where's Naree?"

"I'm here," came his sister's voice from across the chamber. "I've been waiting for you."

Jae and Mayhara exchanged a look.

"Waiting?" Jae asked. "But you've been running from us."

"I only wanted to lead you here," she replied. She lifted the dagger as if inspecting it, and then she tucked it into her belt. "I thought you might wonder if this is where Kashmeru's spirit dwelled."

Mayhara took in the shimmering chamber. She doubted a deity so evil would be buried in a place so beautiful. Beside her, Jae furrowed his brow. He clearly didn't believe it, either.

"It is not," Naree said. "He's not so naïve as to let you find him so easily. But he asked me to get you out of the way. He knows you're trying to stop him. And he won't have it."

If this was not where the body was actually buried, then Mayhara deduced that Naree had only led them there to trick them, to trap them here so she could continue to heed Kashmeru's call.

"Naree, don't do this," Jae said. "Please. It doesn't have to be this way."

Naree shook her head. "I'm sorry. But it does. This is what he wants."

"But it's not what you want." Jae's hands were clenched into fists. "The Lotus always rejects Kashmeru in the end."

"That may be the case," she replied. "And if the same fate is upon him, he will destroy the universe so that every soul can share his pain."

"Naree," Mayhara said, her voice pleading. But Naree didn't look at her. "Lakshmi," she said instead, calling the Lotus by her deity name. "You know not to let this happen. You are the pure one. You must fight back."

Naree only regarded her for a moment, and then she stepped closer, closing the distance between them. "You cannot begin to understand the bond between us. Our souls are from another plane. We were created for each other."

"But you can't let the universe be destroyed," Jae said. "It's up to you to save it."

Naree's palms grew purple. Sadness clouded her face, and she stared intensely at Mayhara. "Mayhara, my crimson mage. You must help me. I'm in peril."

Mayhara stared back at her, her mind buzzing. It was shocking to hear the Lotus empress say her name. She hadn't realized the empress knew it. The empress's palms glowed a bright white, and the emotion Mayhara felt seeping into her pores was unavoidable. She had to protect her. She blinked, trying to keep her thoughts straight, but she found herself losing that battle. Something inside of her needed to listen to the empress.

"Save me, Mayhara!" the Lotus said. "It's your duty to protect me." The Lotus pointed to Jae, fear in her eyes. "The enemy is threatening me."

Across from Mayhara, Jae's face began to change. He

looked back and forth between the Lotus and Mayhara. "No! I'm not the enemy. It's your brother—Jae!"

Mayhara held her hands out, replaying his words in her head. *I'm the enemy. I'm going to kill the Lotus empress.*

Yes, that was what he had said. She was sure of it. Who was this man threatening the empress?

Mayhara turned to him, stepping between him and the empress. She couldn't let her be harmed.

"No, you will not touch her," she shouted, glowing crimson particles emanating from her palms. Scowling, she thrust her energy out. Torrents of granite-like, crimson particles tore through the air toward him.

"No," he yelled. "Don't!"

He tried to defend himself with his sapphire energy, but the crimson rock found its way through, grabbing on to him and adhering to him, forming a stone trap. He shifted, grunting as he attempted to free himself, but it wouldn't budge.

His eyes went to the Lotus, desperation apparent in his voice. "Naree, stop! Stop manipulating her. Please! Don't make her do this."

Naree ignored him. "Protect me, Mayhara. It's your duty!"

Mayhara swung her arm, pitching a glowing crimson sphere toward him. It zoomed through the air and caught him in the chest, knocking him to the ground. More particles attached themselves to him, making the stone trap thicker and heavier.

He clenched his teeth as he raised his palms. Vivid blue energy crystals formed into a sphere. "Mayhara, I don't want to hurt you. Please stop. It's me. Please."

"Don't let him get to me, Mayhara," Naree shouted. "You're my crimson mage! You need to protect me. You need to destroy him!"

Mayhara's eyes widened. "Yes, Empress! As you command." The garnet on her wristband glowed, and she could feel her power intensify. She put one foot forward and hurled crimson energy at the threat. Red, glowing particles rained on the enemy, pinning him down ever more.

He coughed, trying to block the crimson dust with his sapphire energy, but not able to block it all.

"Mayhara, don't do this!" he pleaded. "She's manipulating you!"

Mayhara blinked, his words circling around her, but again she felt the distress of the empress needing her. His words were clearer in her head: *I will kill the Lotus. She will die at my hands.*

Mayhara squared her jaw and thrust her hands out farther, increasing the amount of crimson particles to form around him. It weighed down on him, trapping him, restricting his movement. She had to save her empress. She couldn't let this enemy kill her.

He winced, bringing his hands forward, worming them through the crimson rock. A bright blue glow slowly formed at his palms. He clenched his teeth as he thrust his hands out toward Mayhara.

Tendrils of blue snaked through the air until they finally reached her, swirling around her until they formed a shield of transparent blue fog.

"I'm not your enemy, Mayhara," he said. "It's me. Jae-hyun. Your friend."

This time Mayhara heard it correctly. She gasped and retracted her hands, closing her fingers into her palms and stumbling backward. She blinked, realizing what she had been doing and feeling an acidic sickness in her stomach. She'd almost killed him.

"Oh my God, Jae!" Mayhara's hands flew to her mouth. "I'm… I'm sorry. I thought—"

"No!" Naree yelled. "What are you doing? I told you to destroy him."

Jae pushed at the crimson rock with all his might, but it wouldn't budge. Mayhara reached out and pulled at the air in front of her. The crimson particles fell apart, crumbling to dust at his feet.

Naree raised her hands, palms out, ready to attack again, but Jae threw out his sapphire energy at her. It reached her before she could fight it off.

"Naree, you don't want to hurt us," Jae said. "You shouldn't let Kashmeru control you. You are the pure one. He wants to kill you."

Naree tried to wave off his particles, but they swirled around her, making their way to her ears.

"You love me, Naree. And I love you." Jae stepped closer to her.

She tried to back away, but Mayhara quickly threw out crimson particles and trapped Naree's feet. Naree raised her brows in surprise, looking first at her feet and then back at Jae.

"We're family," Jae said to Naree. "We need to stick together. Please hear me, sister. Please. We need to keep the universe safe."

Naree blinked. She lowered her hands slowly and her expression changed. "Family," she said softly.

"Yes," Jae said, his voice breaking. "Family."

Naree's hands flew to the sides of her head. She pressed in on her temples, looking as if she were waking from a bad dream. Her attention flew to Mayhara.

"Oh no, what have I done?" Naree buckled to her knees, tears streaming down her cheeks. "I… I killed people. I almost killed you both. What has he done to me?"

Mayhara and Jae hurried to her side as she sobbed. Jae wrapped his arms around her, shushing her.

"It'll be all right," he said. "We'll get you somewhere safe and put an end to this."

Naree looked up and him, and with a hiccup, she wrapped her arms around his neck and apologized through her tears.

Jae closed his eyes and squeezed her tightly. When he opened them again, he looked up at Mayhara and reached for her hand. Without making a sound, he mouthed, "Thank you."

Mayhara nodded. With a small smile, she squeezed his hand in return.

Twenty-two

Under Naree's illusion power, the three of them had been able to get back to Jae's place safely. They had all exhausted themselves to the point where all they could do once they had gotten inside the apartment was collapse. Jae sent an encrypted message to Darshana to let her know everything that had happened, but she hadn't responded yet. Mayhara suspected she was in a compromised position and couldn't get back to them right away. Again, they would have to wait.

Jae had insisted Naree take his room. Mayhara had had no objections; after all, this was the Lotus empress they were dealing with. Mayhara had been born to serve her, and as far as Mayhara was concerned, Naree could have any bed in the entire district she wanted.

Mayhara curled up on the couch in a blanket Jae had brought her. She held the dagger in her hand, inspecting its fine grooves and intricate design. It was magical; she could feel it. There was practically a buzzing emanating from within it. It was almost as if it were trying to move, being drawn to someone or someplace where it was destined to be used. It had a purpose.

Jae appeared in front of her and handed her a mug. "Thought we could use something to relax our nerves," he said.

"Thanks."

"She's asleep," he said. "Of course, I keep checking to make sure. It's like part of me doesn't trust that she's really here."

"I know what you mean. And after being under her illusion spell in the caves, it's not that easy to trust anything is real."

Jae took a sip of his tea and then nodded.

They sat quietly for a while, and Mayhara couldn't help but wonder if Jae's mage power of sound included assuring the absence of noise. She would be envious of him if it did. She'd love to be able to shut off the world sometimes, even if just for a few minutes.

"I'm still bummed Bruno's phone got crushed in the crimson," Jae said, leaning back on the couch and scrubbing a hand over his face.

"Sorry about that. My fault."

One corner of his mouth crept upward.

"We still have his computer files," he said. "But the Pishacha could easily change their plans now, and we would be none the wiser."

Mayhara set her tea down on the coffee table and turned to face Jae. "I know this isn't over, and I don't know if anything is ever going to be okay. You've got to be feeling the same restlessness I am. Tell me I'm not wrong."

He pursed his lips for a moment. "You're not wrong. I'm completely on edge, but I can't let it get to me. There's too much riding on this not getting messed up."

"Oh, just the universe," she joked.

Jae smiled at her. "Just that old thing."

They each laughed, and Mayhara felt a small bit of tension fall away. She knew she couldn't go back to her old life. And she didn't want to see the collapse of the universe. As hard as it was for her to accept the fact that she had a hand to play in preventing that collapse, she knew it was the right path to take.

"We're headed in the right direction, right?" she asked. Her stomach fluttered, and there was an expanded feeling in her chest. "I hope that what we've done, getting your sister back, is enough for now."

He took her hand and squeezed it, a softness falling around his eyes. "Even if it's not, we're a team now. Whatever comes our way, we can deal with it together."

⚘

The morning sun filtered in through the living room windows, warming Mayhara's face. She yawned and stretched, pushing herself to a sitting position on the couch. The inviting smell of coffee wafted through the air, bringing a smile to her face.

When she got to her feet, meaning to head to the kitchen, the sight of Jae standing motionless in the corridor caught her eye. He held a small piece of paper in his hand. Her brow furrowed as she approached him.

"What are you doing?"

He looked at her, his mouth pulled into a frown. "Naree is gone. So is the dagger."

It took a moment for Mayhara to wrap her head around what he'd said. "What? When? How?"

He shook his head. "She must have left sometime in the middle of the night. When I got up, the bed was empty."

Mayhara wanted to reach out to Jae, but she reconsidered, figuring he might need his own space to process. They'd been through so much to find her, to get her back safe and out of the hands of the Pishacha, only for her to disappear fewer than twenty-four hours later.

"What's that?" Mayhara asked, pointing to the paper in his hand.

"A letter," he said. "*My beloved Jae-hyun,*" he read, "*I'm sorry to abandon you again, but I cannot escape my destiny. He calls me, so I must go. Though it pains me to leave you,* oppa, *I must follow my path.*"

His hand dropped, and his eyes slowly rose to gaze at Mayhara. She didn't know what to say; she was still trying to wrap her head around the fact that it had happened so quickly.

A knock at the door took them out of their introspection. Mayhara put a hand to her throat, holding back saying out loud that it could be Naree. She didn't want to give Jae any false hope.

Jae hurried to the door. When he opened it, his face remained stoic. He stood back, allowing Darshana to enter the apartment.

"She's gone." His tone proved he couldn't believe it himself.

Darshana clicked her tongue, her expression sad as she placed her hands upon his upper arms. "I'm so sorry. I was afraid the fight might not be over so quickly."

"You knew this would happen?" Mayhara asked.

Darshana walked toward her and stroked her cheek. "No, dear. I'm not a psychic. But I had a feeling either the Pishacha would come hunt her down or Kashmeru would reach her mind somehow. He won't stop calling to her, you know. Not until she either frees him… or kills him."

Mayhara swallowed hard. "So this is just the beginning?"

"We have more information now. We know what we're looking for."

"The daggers," Jae said. "I'm gathering there are seven."

"That would correlate with the legend. The Council of the Seven, the seven mages, the seven chakras, the seven deadly sins…the seven circles of hell."

Mayhara shivered. She and Jae exchanged a look.

"So we need to track down the other six Keys and get the daggers before the Pishacha do," Mayhara said. "But how do we even know where to start?"

Darshana regarded both of them, and Mayhara felt fear wash over her. Her stomach soured and her blood felt as if it were running cold. She was afraid Darshana might not have an answer for them. She was afraid they were lost.

Darshana let out a deep sigh. "I did some meditating while I was laying low. And on my transcendental journey, an image came into my mind. It took me a while to focus on it and figure out what it was. But finally, I did."

Mayhara pressed her palms together and brought her fingers to her lips, waiting for Darshana to continue.

"What was it?" Jae asked, looking as if he were about to jump out of his skin.

Darshana raised a brow. "A scroll. The answer to our problems, once and for all."

TURN THE PAGE

FOR A

PREVIEW OF

COPPER MAGE,

BOOK TWO

IN THE

EMPIRE OF THE LOTUS

SERIES

One

ayhara cringed as she pulled the computer tower from the rubble, her fingers aching from the bite of the jagged pieces of stone. She couldn't use her powers on the stone; the academy building had been enchanted to withstand mage powers so the students wouldn't accidentally destroy it. Even the bricks that made up the building were unable to be penetrated by the magic. But the enchantment had done nothing against the bullets and battering rams the New Asian Administration had used to destroy the school during the Eradication.

With one final yank, she loosened the machine from where it was wedged, but dread overcame her as she took in the damage the casing had endured. She could only hope the hard drive was still intact. They were relying on the information it contained. She was quick to unscrew the casing and disconnect the hard drive. It was crushed in one corner, but she had to think positive—it would work; it would be fine.

With the hard drive in hand, Mayhara stood. Sirens in the distance caused her to freeze in place. She shouldn't be here. She shouldn't be anywhere, actually, except in a prison camp with her family—which was exactly where she'd end up if she was caught sneaking around the demolished mage academy. Instinctively, she backed up against the wall, her long dark hair falling across her face as she ducked her head.

She waited until the sirens faded, her breaths slowing in relief once they'd passed. Wincing, she realized she'd been crushing the hard drive into her chest. Her grip had been too tight, and a drop of blood bloomed against her deep brown complexion She adjusted the hardware and steeled her feelings. The fear of getting caught was not only an issue of getting thrown into a prison camp; if she was captured now, her mission would be jeopardized. And if that happened, it could mean the end of the world.

Holding the hard drive securely, she scanned the room. She wasn't sure there would be anything else of use to her in the administration office of the school. She held what she hoped were the complete files of every student who'd ever attended the academy, but she wasn't confident it was all they would need to track down the other elite mages. At least, the ones who had survived.

She shuddered at the thought of the government's war on mages—and worse, the Pishacha's plan to terminate the elites as a direct order from the vengeful deity, Kashmeru. It was bad enough the Lotus empress had slipped from their grasp, unavoidably heeding Kashmeru's call, but Mayhara also had to deal with the fact that an ancient shadow army was out to kill her.

Deciding the hard drive would be enough, she made her way through the fallen bricks and concrete dust and into the hallway. The setting sun barely offered enough light for her to check if her path was clear. She considered using her mage powers to shine some crimson light but thought better of it. She'd just have to travel carefully.

She made it to the end of the hall and approached the stairway leading down to the main floor. Only a third of the stairs was intact, and she had to use some skillful maneuvering to make her way down. Luckily, her tight jacket and fitted, black jeans made tackling the obstacle a little easier. Once she reached the main floor, her eyes immediately went to the damaged hanging tapestry embroidered with the faces of the past Lotus empresses. Centuries of reincarnations of the deity Lakshmi were displayed along the high walls of the great hall, now partially burnt and torn, destroyed in the crossfire during the Eradication.

The only face missing was Naree's.

That was because her family had kept her hidden for years. No one knew she was the reincarnated Lotus empress aside from her family and Darshana, the empire's finest guru. The New Asian Administration didn't know—or at least they hadn't known. For all Mayhara knew, the administration could have found out. And if Mayhara's suspicions were correct and the administration was under the control of the Pishacha, then the fate of the universe was looking rather bleak.

She walked past the rubble that littered the floor and headed for the library. One of the large, wooden double doors hung partially off its hinges. Inside, desks and bookshelves were strewn about on the mosaic-tiled floor. A gaping hole in the wall let in what little was left of the sunlight, the golden beams shining upon the demolished shelves and shredded books. At the far end of the room, Jae crouched over a metal box on the floor.

"Find anything?" she asked him.

Jae turned his head toward her and dropped whatever was in his hands. "Nothing that helps."

He stood and stretched, rolling out his shoulder. For a moment, Mayhara was transfixed by his lean, muscular form, his confident stance, and the heavy set of his brows as he contemplated the situation. He raked a hand through his dark hair and sighed. When his eyes found her again, she cleared her throat and looked down at the hard drive in her hands. It wasn't the first time she'd found herself staring at him. Spending every day with him over the last few weeks, Mayhara had experienced many moments of a quickened heartbeat if he happened to brush her skin, a tingle in her body when they would share a laugh, and the desire to move closer to him while they worked. But she'd always shaken off the feeling as loneliness, as wanting to be close to someone since her family was imprisoned, or simply being in a situation together that not many others would understand. Besides, she couldn't know how he felt, and as brave as she was fighting off Pishacha, she didn't have the nerve to ask him.

Not that there was any time for that, anyway.

They were on a mission to save Jae's sister, to free the spirit of Lakshmi from the evil grasp of Kashmeru, and to ensure the safety of the universe. She had a family she needed to get out of a prison camp, so she shouldn't have wasted a moment wondering if this guy—this former classmate from the Empire of the Lotus Mage Academy— liked her back. It was trivial.

"I found the hard drive," she said, holding it out. "It looks like it took a blow, but maybe we can salvage what's on it."

He strode toward her and held his hands out. She gave him the hardware and then rested her hands on her hips, focusing on their mission once again.

"No way of telling until we get back to the temple," he said. "But the damage appears minor." He flashed her a smile. "I'm hopeful. Good job."

Mayhara ignored the compliment. "No sign of any scrolls?"

"None like the one Darshana described."

"She said it wouldn't be here. She would have recognized it from her vision if it was a scroll that had been kept at the school."

Jae tapped the hard drive against the palm of his hand. "I know. I figured I'd look anyway, just in—" He stopped, lifting his chin.

He'd heard the crumbling before she had. His sapphire powers at work.

With a gasp, Mayhara threw her hands up into the air past Jae's head. A section of the ceiling fell apart, taking with it a metal light fixture that made a direct drop toward where they stood. Quick to use her mage powers, Mayhara released streams of crimson energy, the particles rushing between Jae and the falling debris. The crimson shield solidified, forming a slanted wall that deflected the debris. Her garnet wristband glowed brightly. She pushed out her power until the wall connected sturdily with the floor. As soon as her palms were clear from the crimson dust, Mayhara pulled Jae toward her.

Dust flew around their heads, both from the destroyed ceiling and Mayhara's crimson wall. Jae gaped at how close he had been to getting hit, and then he turned back to Mayhara. They were mere inches apart.

"Are you all right?" she asked.

It took him a moment to respond. He swallowed visibly. "Yes. Thanks."

She averted her eyes. "Yeah, of course."

Her hands were still on his arms. She let them drop, then pushed her hair out of her face, taking a step back. Jae's eyes narrowed slightly, but as he opened his mouth to speak, a buzzing interrupted him.

He pulled his Linq out of his pocket but didn't look long at the screen. "It's Darshana."

"Has she found something out?"

"She didn't say. She just wants us to get back as soon as we can."

Mayhara nodded once. "Then let's go."

READ MORE OF COPPER MAGE

AVAILABLE NOW

From Snowy Wings Publishing

Acknowledgements

I've gone and done it again. I started a new series, created new characters that I can't let go of, and have become invested in their world. This story has been brewing in my mind for a while, and I just hope I can do it justice.

As usual, I have a great writing community to thank for keeping me motivated, as well as friends and family who cheer me on. A special thanks to my ARC team—especially Kalli Bunch for your more-than-generous assistance. You guys rock!

This story is the one that was included in the Cursed Lands boxed set which landed me a spot on the USA Today bestseller list, so I'd like to thank all my set mates, especially Heather Marie Adkins and Rebecca Hamilton for everything they did for us.

And thank you, Kirsten, for the awesome cover!

About the Author

Dorothy Dreyer is a Philippine-born American living in Germany with her husband, her two college kids, and two Siberian Huskies. She is an award-winning, *USA Today* Bestselling Author of young adult and new adult books that usually have some element of magic or the supernatural in them. Her repertoire also includes adult romance and thriller novels. Aside from reading, she enjoys movies, binge-watching series, chocolate, take-out, traveling, and having fun with friends and family.

You can find out more about Dorothy on her website: http://dorothydreyer.com

Also From
Snowy Wings Publishing

When Darkness Whispers

by Heather L. Reid

Kill Me Once, Kill Me Twice

by Clara Kensie

All the Tales We Tell

by Annie Cosby

Find them and more at

https://www.snowywingspublishing.com/books